Festival for
Three
Thousand
Maidens

Festival for Three Thousand Maidens

by
Richard Wiley

A DUTTON BOOK

DUTTON
Published by the Penguin Group
Penguin Books USA Inc., 375 Hudson Street,
New York, New York 10014, U.S.A.
Penguin Books Ltd, 27 Wrights Lane, London W8 5TZ, England
Penguin Books Australia Ltd, Ringwood, Victoria, Australia
Penguin Books Canada Ltd, 2801 John Street,
Markham, Ontario, Canada L3R 1B4
Penguin Books (N.Z.) Ltd, 182–190 Wairau Road,
Auckland 10, New Zealand

Penguin Books Ltd, Registered Offices:
Harmondsworth, Middlesex, England

First published by Dutton, an imprint of New American Library,
a division of Penguin Books USA Inc.
Distributed in Canada by McClelland & Stewart Inc.

First Printing, February, 1991
10 9 8 7 6 5 4 3 2 1

For permission to reprint the song lyrics in this novel, grateful acknowl-
edgment is made to the following:
   Aria Music Company for "Too Young."
   "Love Potion #9," © 1959 (renewed) Jerry Leiber Music, Mike Stoller
   Music, all rights reserved. Used by permission.
   Winwood Music Co., Inc. for "Coffee Blues" as written by John Hurt,
   copyright 1963, 1976 by Winwood Music Co., Inc. All rights reserved.
   Used by permission.

 REGISTERED TRADEMARK—MARCA REGISTRADA

LIBRARY OF CONGRESS CATALOGING-IN-PUBLICATION DATA:
Wiley, Richard.
   Festival for three thousand maidens / by Richard Wiley.
      p.   cm.
I. Title.
PS3573.I433F45   1991
813'.54—dc20   90-44044
                                                                              CIP

Printed in the United States of America
Designed by Eve L. Kirch

For my first family,
Kenneth, Alice,
and Tad

Thanks to John and Kay Duncan for answering my questions about Korea, to John Cushing, Dan Denerstein, Charles DeWolf and Joe Nowakowski for their stories, and to that preternatural group, K-3, for being what they were.

AUTHOR'S NOTE

The chapter headings in this book have been selected (nearly) at random from the *I Ching*, the ancient Confucian *Book of Changes*, which is called *Yuk Kyong* in Korean. In the old days when someone wanted to consult the *I Ching*, yarrow stalks were cast, and the caster, by using the arrangement of broken and unbroken lines that he found in the stalks was able to form one of sixty-four hexagrams that could be read as an oracle. Once the hexagram was secured, one merely had to look it up in the *Book of Changes* and read what was written, taking from it bits of wisdom that might shed light on the original question, the situation at hand.

Since I didn't have yarrow stalks, I used U.S. pennies for my castings. I kept the essence of each chapter firmly in mind and then asked the following question: "What could I write at the beginning of this chapter that would shed light on the events within?" Thus my chapter headings were secured. The actual chapter titles, above the hexagrams, are merely the names of the hexagrams from the *I Ching*.

Only once did I have to cast my pennies twice, and only once did I come up with the same hexagram for two chapters. When that happened, I cheated a bit, simply choosing a hexagram that I liked, something I remembered reading when glancing through the book at my leisure.

PREFACE

The vice-headmaster's retirement party is held in a judo
hall, where there are flowers at the entrance, big round
displays of them, with Chinese slogans running down
their ribbons, expressing good luck. The floor of the hall
is covered with sheets and the windows are opened to
allow a breeze.

The vice-headmaster comes in from a side door, su-
perbly dressed and wearing a horsehair hat. His face is
well shaven and the troublesome hairs of his nose and
ears have been trimmed back. The vice-headmaster's family takes up the entire front of the hall, and when his
other guests are settled, he kneels beneath a photograph
of the founder of the judo hall, and the headmaster comes
from that same side door in order to begin his speech.
The headmaster does not speak of the vice-headmaster
as an individual, but speaks instead of the five Confucian
relationships: a man to his king, a man to his son, a man
to his wife, a man to his younger brother, and a man to
his friend. Outside of these five relationships, the head-

master asks, what is there left to contemplate? He says that, current trends in the society notwithstanding, there is little room for the man himself, alone and untethered to others, nor should there be an accommodation for anything unconcerned with the betterment and maintenance of these five relationships. The headmaster says that for a man to succeed in life he must remember the hierarchy of attachments. He also says that the vice-headmaster's life has been exemplary.

The headmaster speaks for an hour and all the while the vice-headmaster remains motionless, his demeanor unchanged. The back of the judo hall holds a table that is covered with food and beer, but even when the long speech is finished no one moves, and when the vice-headmaster stands, everyone looks forward to his reply.

"I would like to sing a song in honor of Mr. Bobby, our American friend who is now gone," says the vice-headmaster. He then removes a folded fan from his belt, holding it to his lips as if it were a microphone.

> "Gone are the days
> When my heart was young and gay,
> Gone are the friends
> From the cotton fields away,
> Gone from the earth
> To a better land I know. . . ."

Here the lyrics desert the vice-headmaster, forcing an embarrassed silence, until Mr. Nam's voice is heard, coming from the middle of the room. Mr. Nam knows the chorus of the song well, and as he sings the vice-headmaster remembers the lyrics again and lets his voice trail after Mr. Nam's, like an echo.

> "I'm coming (I'm coming), I'm coming (I'm coming),
> For my head is bending low.

I hear their gentle voices calling
Old Black Joe."

When the song ends the vice-headmaster stands, silently leaning forward. He then remembers himself and, nodding toward his eldest son, gives instructions that his guests should move toward the food and drink at the back of the room.

Part One

When the headmaster announced today that an American teacher would be joining our staff, there was, on the face of it, a good deal of happy anticipation, but there was skepticism as well. The skepticism came about, I believe, because we have always been a self-contained group, each understanding the weaknesses of the others and content to pass our days without ruffling feathers. In other words, we all have our niches, and we aren't at all sure there is an extra niche for the American.

But during the morning meeting, particularly when the headmaster was in the room, happy anticipation was the face we gave our fears. Think of it, we all gushed, an American teaching in our school! Since my job as vice-headmaster seemed to call for it, I asked, "What does the American look like," but what I really wanted to ask was, "What in the world will we do with him, how will we relate to him except as an outsider, and how will we communicate except in Korean?"

I know that by admitting such concerns I am unmasking myself as one of the skeptics. And though I am sure Headmaster Kim knows what he is doing, the announcement made me nervous and oddly sad, as if the end of our natural order of things were at hand.

Ah well, the headmaster said that the American will be staying for two years, a period of time that extends beyond my own retirement and *hwangap*, so when the American leaves, I'll be gone too—he back to his own place, me off to grow my beard.

When the American arrives, however, I have resolved to look into his face in the hope that I will see some inroad there, some path. If I do, one of these days I shall speak to him. If I do not, I shall not. If I were a younger man I might look upon this arrival with a feeling more akin to pleasure, but since I am not young, my further resolution is this: I shall comport myself like a *yangban* when this American is about. After all, if I have lived my life in a dignified manner until now, what other choice do I have?

Written at my desk, long after the other teachers have left for the day.

4300 年　10 月　　2 日

The Wanderer

≡≡ ≡≡

Six in the second place means: The wanderer
comes to an inn, he has his property with him.
He wins the steadfastness of a young servant.

B obby Comstock had spent most of the days of
his life going from hungry to stuffed, and when
he and Mr. Soh, an English teacher who'd been sent to
Seoul to bring him down the coast, stepped onto the
platform at Taechon village, he was not only hungry, but
nervous as well. Would they like him? Would they be
offended by how fat he was? He was met by a line of
dignitaries, neatly dressed men, all bowing down. Bobby
had studied Korean during his training course, but it had
been far easier to feel sure of himself in a classroom in
America than on the cold station platform of this dark
little town. Still, he was about to speak first, about to
introduce himself, when Mr. Soh shouted in his ear,
frightening his nervousness away. "This is Mr. Bobby
from America!"

Mr. Soh then turned Bobby in the direction of the tallest
man in the group. "Mr. Bobby, this is Headmaster Kim!"

"Hello there," Bobby said, "*Anyanghashimnika.*"

Bobby and Mr. Soh were the only people to get off in

9

Taechon, and when the train pulled away, the dignitaries ushered them out onto a dark, poorly lit street. There was a cart man nearby, and Mr. Soh told him to get Bobby's trunk from the platform and follow along.

Headmaster Kim said something and Mr. Soh translated.

"You must be tired," he said.

It was only nine o'clock but Bobby's greatest desire, quite suddenly, was to be alone, so he said slowly in Korean, "I am tired, yes. Tired from my long trip. Tired from all those weeks of study in America."

Headmaster Kim nodded, but he had something else on his mind. They had been walking up the dim street— the town seemed completely closed though Bobby did notice the sign for a tearoom or two—and had come to a shabby building at the edge of town. "I do not yet have a home for you," said the headmaster. "No one who will take you in. I will soon find someone, but in the meantime I must put you up at this inn."

The headmaster was anxious; the agreement had been that all Peace Corps volunteers would live with Korean families, but Bobby was relieved. This would give him time to himself, time to get used to his teaching load and to begin his further study of Korean, before having to worry about a family.

The inn they had chosen for him was one of two in the village and after he agreed to stay in it, Headmaster Kim and the others bid him good night. Mr. Soh stayed until Bobby was shown to his room, a rectangle so small that he would have to sleep diagonally on the floor, but then Mr. Soh hurried away too, leaving Bobby in the hands of a boy who worked at the inn. This boy had a dirty face and cold sores so crowded his upper lip that from a distance he looked like Charlie Chaplin. The boy was called 'Goma,' a word that means midget in Korean, and after

Mr. Soh left he brought Bobby a bowl of cold rice and sat in the corner of the room.

"I'm not hungry," said Bobby, looking at the rice.

"I'll take it," said the boy. "Hand it over."

The single bulb that lit the room was no more than forty watts strong, but the Goma's scabby lip was highlighted in it. Bobby tried to speak to the boy while he polished off the rice.

"How many people live in this town?" he asked. His Korean was halting, but he was sure the sentence was correct.

"Search me," said the Goma.

"Where's the toilet? How many rooms are there in this inn?"

He had used a high-class word for toilet and the Goma laughed. "No such room," he said. "Only a stinking hole in the floor."

Bobby hadn't understood the boy's responses but he smiled anyway, and just then his Peace Corps trunk was delivered by the cart man.

"What's that?" asked the Goma.

Bobby opened the trunk and looked at his clothing folded there. Underneath the top layer were a few gifts he had bought, little things to give to people he happened to meet, and he pulled out a fingernail clipper, handing it to the boy.

"This is something small I brought you from America," he said.

The Goma took the fingernail clipper in his filthy hands, and while he examined it Bobby took out a photograph of his grandmother, the woman who had raised him since the early death of his parents, and a sack of chocolate-chip cookies. He had told the Goma he wasn't hungry, but when he saw the cookies his hunger came back. He ate ten of them and then handed one to the Goma, carefully tucking the remaining thirteen back into his trunk. The Goma put the cookie and the fingernail clipper in the left front pocket of his awful pants.

It was an inauspicious beginning but Bobby could not be bothered by that. Later, he tried to tell the Goma to leave so that he could lie down on his bedding and sleep. He had intended to write his grandmother, but such an activity would put off sleep for too long, and he wanted to be fresh for his first day of teaching come tomorrow. The Goma, however, seemed content to stay where he was, and though Bobby tried several of his memorized Korean sentences, nothing he said could make the boy leave.

"Go!" he said, finally. "Get out of here now!" This was a single line of street Korean that a favorite teacher of his had taught him, and the Goma jumped.

"OK, fatso," he said, "have it your way."

Bobby understood only the tone of what the Goma said, but when the kid was halfway around the inn's courtyard, Bobby nevertheless stuck his head back through the door of his room and called after him, wanting to make things right. "It was a pleasure meeting you," he said, and though he could not be sure, he thought he heard the Goma belch out of the darkness from the other side of the inn.

Peace

Nine at the beginning means: When ribbon grass is pulled up, the sod comes with it. Each according to his kind.

As it happened, Bobby Comstock's first day at Taechon Boys' Middle School was a Friday, and not much was going on. When he and Mr. Soh walked through the school gate the students crowded around them, and there was an interminable welcoming meeting in the teachers' room—run by the vice-headmaster, Headmaster Kim was gone—but Bobby hadn't understood what was said, and by the time he met his first class he was already tired from being so much on stage, and ready for a nap.

Still, he tried to teach well; he made the students laugh with various contortions of his cheeks and tongue, and by the end of the day he wanted only to go back to his room to sleep. After all, he had just arrived, and his internal clock was racing; not only was it way after midnight in America, but the discovery that the teachers all brought their lunches to school had shocked him. Mr. Soh, to be sure, had found a lunch for Bobby, but by quitting time it was the idea that he would soon be alone in his room and could open up the lid of his Peace Corps trunk that drew him.

Mr. Soh, however, had other ideas. "Come," he said. "You may have noticed that Headmaster Kim was gone today."

It was five o'clock and they were walking across the playground on their way back into town.

"What's wrong?" Bobby asked. "I hope the headmaster isn't ill?"

"No," said his fellow English teacher, "but Headmaster Kim's relative has died and we must now attend the funeral."

Mr. Soh had learned his English during the Korean War, and it wasn't as bad as Bobby had thought on the train. Mr. Soh could, after all, speak fairly well, but he had a difficult time understanding anything Bobby said to him. He'd been a KATUSA during the war, a Korean Attached to the United States Army, and he still hated the North. Other than English teaching, he liked to say, anticommunism was his consuming passion.

Parked outside the school gate was a small Volkswagen bus, one that Mr. Soh had been able to borrow. Inside the bus several other teachers sat, the vice-headmaster among them, but Bobby didn't recall any of their names.

"Hello," they all said, "sit near the driver," and when Mr. Soh got into the driver's seat, Bobby slipped in behind him, smiling at everyone, determined to try to act pleased with the prospect of attending a funeral on his second night in town, though the seat was too small and he had his fat knees up under his chin. And, indeed, though the village of Taechon was primitive enough in itself, with no truly paved streets, they were soon climbing into the hills on pathways so rutted that it seemed the little bus might fall over onto its side. The afternoon sun had already fallen behind the edge of a hill, but when Bobby noticed a slim moon hanging opposite it, his spirits did rise. He opened the window slightly and breathed in the cool country air. This was no time for fatigue. The people around him would be his friends and coworkers for the next two years. He could sleep later, when the time for camaraderie had run its course.

Mr. Soh spent part of the journey teaching Bobby how to say "Please accept my condolences" in Korean, and when they finally parked the bus he had it down. Mr. Soh waited until the dust had settled before opening the door, and when they got out the teachers led Bobby quickly into the rice fields, along a narrow path. "Please watch your step," someone said. "The fields are thick with fertilizer."

Bobby nodded, but he had begun to wonder how he should behave at this funeral. Was he to act sad, as he would in America? He was not unfamiliar with funerals, but he nevertheless wanted to ask someone, to settle a few points before they arrived. And though the turns of the path and the way the others kept their eyes on the ground made him hold his tongue, he soon began experimenting with a downcast expression around his eyes.

When they entered the yard Mr. Soh cleared his throat. "We are here," he said quietly, and an old woman who'd been tending the fire stopped what she was doing and hurried over to them. Ignoring the teachers completely, she got down on her hands and knees and began bowing in front of Bobby.

"Do what she does," Mr. Soh said, so Bobby dropped to the ground too, the flesh on his back and arms bouncing with the impact.

"Thank you for honoring us with your attendance at this funeral," said the old woman.

"Please accept my condolences," said Bobby.

He had delivered the sentence well, and the old woman rolled out of her bow, looking up. "What did you say?" she asked.

"Please accept my condolences," Bobby said again.

"Well, I never . . . !" said the old woman. "Hey everybody! Junior's friend speaks perfect Korean! Come listen."

Mr. Soh was translating for him when five or six others moved forward and the woman told Bobby to speak again.

"Please accept my condolences," he repeated.

"You see. What did I tell you? Perfect Korean!"

They all agreed and said that they were glad to meet him and thanked him for honoring the dead woman with his attendance at the funeral.

"That was fine," said Mr. Soh, "you are doing well." The other teachers had drifted away, but Mr. Soh led Bobby around to the smallest room of the house where they removed their shoes and crawled in through a rice-paper door. "Here she is," said Mr. Soh. "Headmaster Kim's uncle's wife's cousin."

A photograph in a dark frame was propped on an altar in the center of the room. Candles circled the photograph, and behind it, in a wooden box, was the actual body of the cousin herself, a woman in her late sixties.

Mr. Soh knelt on a cushion in front of the photograph and bowed. "She was a Christian," he said, "but a Buddhist too. Auntie wants us to honor both religions." Mr. Soh was a shirttail relative of Headmaster Kim, and when he pulled Bobby up to the coffin they both gazed down at the woman, who reclined there in a way that seemed nearly casual, though at the same time her face was so unrestful that Bobby thought that she might, at any moment, sit up. It was a thought he'd had at other funerals, and it made him remember his grandmother. Would she die while he was away? Should he have stayed at home, where he could see her again and again before the end of her life, where he could watch her in her coffin, waiting for her to make a move?

Mr. Soh's aunt opened the outside door, chasing such thoughts away. "Hurry, Junior," she said. "There is food and drink in the other room. Take your friend in there. There is a chair. We've even found a chair for him." She turned to the women in the yard behind her. "Foreigners use chairs," she let them know.

Once outside again Mr. Soh led Bobby over to another door, where they crawled into the main room of the house. This room wasn't any larger than the first, but it was a little better looking, with a thick yellow *ondol* floor. Korean floors are heated by charcoal fires from under the house, and though the floor at Bobby's inn was faulty, hot in one place and cold in another, this one was evenly heated and soothing under their hands and feet. The teachers who'd come with them on the bus were already in the room, spaced around a long low table. Headmaster Kim was there, seated next to a very old man, and next to the old man, with a soft cushion upon its seat, was a high, stiff-backed chair.

"I know that your aunt is trying to be kind, but I don't want the chair," Bobby said softly, but since the old lady was standing in the doorway, he smiled over his shoulder at her and sat down. Everyone was staring up at him and soon the headmaster said something that included his name. An introduction, apparently, to his uncle.

"Nice to meet you," Bobby said.

"She was right," said the old man. "You speak Korean well." He then handed Bobby a full bowl of a rice wine, called makkoli. The old man said, "Drink it, it's good."

Bobby was too aware of his high position in the room to relax, but he put the bowl to his lips and took a small sip.

"Not that way," said the old man. "Drink it all." He pantomimed drinking out of a bowl, then sat up straight, staring and waiting.

"You must drink everything and give him back his bowl," Mr. Soh said. "It is the Korean way."

Though Bobby did not want to, he drank all the makkoli, which was chalky and sour and strong. He handed the bowl back to the old man and filled it from a large copper pot, just like he'd been told to do in training. Bobby wasn't much of a drinker but he told the old man that the wine was good. He was trying to think of something else to say when suddenly Headmaster Kim sat up straight and spoke for him, turning to look down the table at the other guests. "I-don't-speak-English!" he said. A stream of wine was running from the corner of the headmaster's mouth as he spoke and the others laughed. "I-don't-speak-English!" they echoed.

Just then the old woman came back into the room so Bobby took the opportunity to stand up. Mr. Soh came to his aid.

"Auntie, he wants to sit on the floor," he said. "He's cold up there and wants to be closer to the heat."

"Ah ha, he's cold," said the aunt. She looked at the old man harshly, as if the whole idea had been his, and then she said, "Chairs defeat the purpose of a Korean floor." Bobby quickly sat down with the others.

"But don't you find it tiring to sit cross-legged?" the old man asked.

Mr. Soh translated, but Bobby ignored him. He had already composed something else to say. "This makkoli is very good," he answered.

"Our cousin made the best makkoli in the area. This makkoli is inferior. It is paradoxical, don't you think, that we must drink inferior makkoli at her funeral?"

Mr. Soh again helped with the translation, but he was irritated. It was he who had bought the makkoli, driving up and down the mountain late the night before, after Bobby's arrival.

The old woman and two younger ones came back into the room, carrying large plates of rice and various side dishes of *kimchi* and dried fish. One heaping plate of beef was placed directly in front of Bobby.

"That's *pulgogi*," said Mr. Soh. "It's our best dish."

The meat was delicious, but Bobby tried to eat slowly, mindful that they were all watching. And though Mr. Soh still sat next to him, he was now leaning the other way. His English was drowning in the wine but his Korean was riding above it, joining the voices of the others in shouts and epitaphs and snatches of song.

Bobby had begun to drift a little, amazed to be involved in something so foreign to what he knew, but he was jarred when the old man gave him a strong nudge. Headmaster Kim was sitting with an empty bowl in his hands, staring, so Bobby finished his drink and handed his own bowl past the old man. The headmaster bowed while Bobby filled it, then handed it back after he'd quickly drained it all. Now bowls were being exchanged all along the table, makkoli drunk and spilled on the floor and down the shirts of all the men. The old man pinched Bobby's sleeve and asked, "How old are you?"

"I'm twenty-three," Bobby answered, happy to have understood.

"He's twenty-three!" the old man announced. "He's the youngest among us, he's everyone's younger brother!" and though Bobby understood the words, he also remembered having been told in training that being the youngest among Korean men was no honor.

The old woman came back again and sat down at the far end of the table.

"Good," said the old man, "the women are here. It is now time to begin our singing."

"The foreigner should sing first," the old woman told him. "It is the polite thing to do."

But the old man frowned. "No, the foreigner should sing last," he said. "*That* is the polite thing to do. Where did you learn your manners? You sing first, set the proper tone."

Bobby had only a vague idea of what was going on

but he put it together when the old woman picked up her chopsticks and began beating on the table in front of her.

"Auntie is going to sing," said Mr. Soh, but the old man told him to shut up.

" 'A-ri-rang, a-ri-rang, a-ra-di-yo,' " crooned the old woman. "A-ri-rang, co-o ge-e rul nomu gan da.' "

After she'd sung the first line of the song the others joined in. They were all beating on their bowls or on the table itself, swaying with the music.

" 'Na dul po-ri-go ka shi-nun-nim-u-u-un, shim-ni-do mo-ca-so pal pyong na da.' "

When the old woman finished, everyone applauded. "That was 'Arirang,' " said the old man. "It is the greatest Korean song." He eyed the old woman again and then turned to Mr. Soh. "Now the foreigner should sing," he said. "Tell him to sing something we all know. How about 'Delilah!' We'd love to hear that one."

But before Mr. Soh could speak or Bobby could respond, Headmaster Kim came alive again. "No!" he said, "I've got it. 'Love Potion Number Nine!' Tell him to sing 'Love Potion Number Nine!' "

Bobby looked at them all and thought of America, the home of such songs, a million miles away. His vision was blurred as he picked up his chopsticks and lightly hit the edge of his wine bowl the way the old woman had.

" 'I took my troubles down to Madam Ruth. . . .' " he said softly, but the old man took hold of his arm.

"You mustn't talk," the old man explained. "Sing. This is singing we are talking about here and this is the time for a song."

Bobby smiled at the old man, almost rolling his tongue around inside his mouth like he'd done with the students earlier in the day. He would never sing such a song in America, but what the hell. . . . No one knew him here. He took a deep breath then and really did begin to sing, the lyrics unleashed from some dormant depository in his brain.

" 'I took my troubles down to Madam Ruth. . . .' "

"Cha-cha-cha," said the old man.

" 'You know that gypsy with the gold-capped tooth. . . .' "

"Cha-cha-cha."

" 'She looked at me and she made a little sign. She said what you need is . . .' "

" 'Love Potion Number Na-a-a-a-ine,' " sang everyone in the room.

Something in Bobby broke loose then and he laughed, the flesh around his neck and shoulders moving with the laughter and the song. Music was the international language and he sang loudly, proud of every word.

" 'She jumped down turned around and gave me a wink. . . . She said I'm gonna mix it up right here in the sink. . . .' " About half the people in the room were singing along now.

" 'It tastes like turpentine, it smells like India ink. . . .' "

"Cha-cha-cha," said the old man.

" 'I held my nose, I closed my eyes. . . .' " Bobby bellowed acappella, holding his nose and closing his eyes.

" 'I took a drink. . . .' " sang the old man, and they all continued.

" 'I didn't know if it was day or night. . . .' "

"CHA-CHA-CHA."

" 'I started kissing everything in sight. . . .' "

"CHA-CHA-CHA."

Bobby and the old man were watching each other and singing high up in their lungs. The table was bouncing up and down and everyone was swaying.

" 'But when I kissed the cop down at Thirty-fourth and Vine . . . He broke my little bottle of . . .' "

" 'Love Potion Number Naaaine,' " they all sang loudly.

" 'Love Potion Number Naaaine,' " they sang a bit softer.

" 'Love Potion Number Na-a-a-a-ine!' " This last line they sang quite softly, holding the final note until finally everyone had to take another breath.

"CHA-CHA-CHA!" they all screamed, then they threw their chopsticks up into the air and fell, drunk and laughing, across the floor.

The old man recovered first. He sat up, patted Bobby's arm, then filled two bowls with wine.

"Congratulations," said Mr. Soh, "you've made a great impression on my uncle. He now wants to give you something."

"I will compose a poem," said the old man. "Everybody listen. I will compose a poem for our younger brother."

Everyone was leaning forward, red-faced. They tried to remain quiet but could not.

"Shut up!" the old man ordered. "Have you no respect for age?" He quieted and looked at Bobby again. "This is a summer poem, in honor of the coming winter," he said. "Its purpose is to tide you over until we meet again."

Bobby was swaying back and forth, smiling as if he understood. His cheeks were burning and his mouth was wet and he could see only the old man's thin face, beside him like a crescent moon.

"All right, I've got it," the old man said. "Everybody listen." He was quiet again, but then he erupted in a strange, monotonous tone, his stark voice tearing at the momentary calm:

> "Flies on the table—
> We sat drinking makkoli—
> With flies in it."

The old man leaned over, his eyes inches from Bobby's. Everybody in the room was waiting for his reaction.

"Flies on the table, we sat drinking makkoli, with flies in it," said Mr. Soh.

Bobby stared at them all and then swallowed and tried to think of a Korean word to say. Mr. Soh was breathing heavily at his side, but though Bobby looked at the table and smiled, no words came. Finally the old man poked him and Bobby looked up one more time.

"Please accept my condolences," he said.

The dinner ended when one of the women flung the paper doors aside, driving them all out into the night. Those who lived nearby walked to the edge of the court-yard and stepped onto the small footpaths, staggering into the darkness. But for some reason Bobby stumbled over to the room containing the dead woman's body once more. He slid the door open and climbed in and crawled across the floor to the table-altar and took the photograph down, trying to look at it in the bit of moon-light that had followed him in. And he slipped the pho-tograph inside his jacket when he heard the others calling his name.

Those who remained included the old man, the head-master, and those who had come on the bus. The old woman was pulling on the old man's arm. "Piss on the curfew," she said. "Our cousin does not die every day. Stay and drink. Stay and sing. We must keep her company."

But the old man jerked away, hopping into the side of the house. "Let's go, Junior," he said, and the old woman, sensing defeat, fell to the ground in front of Bobby again.

"Thank you for coming," she said. "Thank you for honoring us by coming to the funeral of our cousin."

They all began bowing to the old lady, backing out of the yard. Mr. Soh went first, brandishing a big flashlight and shining it back and forth along the path. The night was gray, then black, then gray again as clouds moved across the moon. It was cold and all the men soon pulled their heads into their overcoats and became silent.

Bobby could feel the dead woman's photograph pressing into his flesh, and wanted to turn around and take it back. He had no idea why he'd taken it, yet even in his drunkenness he was sure that they would miss it soon, that someone would come along, asking for its return. He turned around to look at the others, to try to make some excuse, but when he did so he slipped off the path. Quickly his legs disappeared into the muck, one to its knee, the other all the way up to his crotch. He shouted and tried to pull himself free, but it was no good. The Koreans gathered around. They pulled him from the muck laughing, all of them staggering about but somehow staying on the path.

"He's too drunk," said the old man. "We must carry him." He was gesturing wildly but no one wanted to get close to Bobby's legs, and in another few strides they were on the dirt road, standing beside the dark bus.

"I am sorry," said Headmaster Kim, but when Mr. Soh opened the bus door he climbed on quickly, sitting down in the seat Bobby had previously used, the one directly behind the driver's.

Bobby sat opposite Headmaster Kim, and the old man squeezed onto the seat with him, moving quickly past his knees so that he could sit by the window. "Koreans can hold their liquor," he chuckled. "You fell off the path. Phew! Your leg smells like ox shit." The Koreans all smiled, but the old man leaned into Bobby then, helping him pull his pantlegs away from his body with his strong old fingers.

Mr. Soh started the engine and drove off while everyone was talking, but as soon as his driving got bad they all sat still. Mr. Soh, with his hat pulled down over his ears, gripped the wheel with both hands and bit his lower lip. The van careened off the mountain road and onto the flat one that led into the village. Once they were on level ground again Headmaster Kim stood and took off the baggy farmer's pants that he was wearing, holding them up in the aisle of the bus like a surrender flag.

"Here," he said in English. "Dry pants . . ." He tossed them to the old man, who immediately began plucking at Bobby's belt. "No time for continuity of dress," he said. "Not where ox shit is concerned."

Bobby held the pants away from him for a moment, ready to argue, but then he stood up awkwardly from the seat and, head bent along the roof, stripped his heavy trousers away. When he let go of them they slumped beside him in the aisle. He quickly slipped into the head-master's baggy pants and felt them blow against his legs in the breeze that came from the door. And when he sat back down again he saw his knees next to the old man's. His soiled trousers still had not completely fallen but had turned in the aisle and were inching forward, up next to Mr. Soh now at the front of the bus. Bobby looked at Headmaster Kim to thank him, but the headmaster was asleep, his naked legs moving with the bends in the road.

Suddenly, as Mr. Soh turned a corner too abruptly, the bus rolled into a stack of discarded boxes and stopped. Bobby's trousers fell, wounded in the aisle. Mr. Soh smiled and opened the door. Somehow they were in front of the inn.

"Good-bye," said the old man.

Bobby stood and tried to think of something appropriate to say, but finally he just climbed down out of the van, pulling his filthy trousers behind him. Headmaster Kim's was the only voice he recognized as Mr. Soh searched for reverse. The headmaster had woken from his doze and was sitting up a little. "I am sorry," he said, and then they backed out of the debris and sped away into the night.

Though the inn was behind him and the night was

cold, Bobby turned into the marketplace, through the broken stalls and down a rutted pathway. He hadn't gone very far before some street children came out of the doorways where they slept and began following along. He took the dead woman's photograph from his jacket, wiped the front of it on the headmaster's pants, and tilted it up so that he could see her face. She was proud in the photograph, nearly arrogant, nothing like his grandmother at all. Bobby stopped at the center of a small bridge. Below him was a dried-up streambed, and as he looked down, the children shuffled in around him, plucking at his jacket and trying to get a look at the photograph. To Bobby's surprise the Goma from the inn was among them. "Hello," the Goma said softly. "Hey you, OK." It was, so far as he knew, the standard American greeting, and when Bobby looked at him, his scab mustache parted in a smile.

As Bobby looked at the woman's photograph he could see the hills beyond it, and he imagined the sea beyond the hills and America over there, somewhere beyond the sea. God, what a night this had been. At the funerals of his parents he had marched carefully past their caskets, head bowed, tears welling in his eyes. That was the way funerals were supposed to be anywhere in the world, any fool knew that. Yet tonight he had gotten drunk and sung unconnected songs, and now he was stuck with this goddamn photograph, staring at him from the bridge railing like the photograph of a judge. He should have taken it back but now it was too late. He had felt like an outcast in America to be sure, but what did he feel here, standing drunkenly in the market like he was?

The Goma tried to take his hand, but when Bobby pulled away he stood back, content to wait for a sign that Bobby was tired and finally ready to go home.

Gathering Together

*Nine in the second place means: If one is sincere
it furthers one to bring even a small offering.*

The Monday after the funeral Bobby went to
school tentatively, the woman's photograph in
a paper sack next to his lunch. Headmaster Kim was in
his office and the teachers were in the teachers' room
when he arrived, so he went directly to the headmaster's
door and knocked.

"Enter," said Headmaster Kim.

"Good morning, sir," said Bobby. "The photograph of
your uncle's wife's cousin is in this sack."

Headmaster Kim did not look up, but since Bobby had
devoted most of his Sunday to learning his lines for this
encounter, he knew they were correct.

"Pardon me?" said the headmaster.

"The photograph of your uncle's wife's cousin is in this
sack."

Although the words were right, the headmaster wasn't
understanding. Bobby had practiced this sentence dozens
of times on the Goma. What was the problem, then, with
the headmaster?

Bobby removed his lunch and laid the sack on the desk, bowing so that the headmaster would think he was contrite.

"Oh," said Headmaster Kim. "Thank you very much."

He took the sack but did not open it, and Bobby realized that the headmaster thought it was a gift Bobby'd brought with him from America. Bobby bowed again and walked back into the teachers' room where the morning meeting was about to begin. Were some of the teachers looking at him strangely? Were these the teachers who had been at the funeral and were they now telling the others what he'd done? Was stealing a dead woman's photo some sort of sacrilege at a Confucian funeral? Bobby wished he were back in training where there were people who could answer questions such as these. He wished he hadn't taken the photograph, of course, and he wished he knew why he had. But when the meeting began he sat down at his desk, losing himself in the drone of language, letting it take him and letting it lessen the already abating feeling that he'd gotten off on the wrong foot.

The official name of the school was Taechon Boys' Middle School and, though it was essentially a nonacademic school—students here ended their education after ninth grade—there were three English teachers besides Bobby: Mr. Soh, Mr. Nam, and Mr. Kwak. Of the three, Mr. Soh appeared to be the only one who spoke decent English. Mr. Nam, however, would not admit that his English was bad, and Mr. Kwak seemed so embarrassed by the fact that he spoke so poorly that he would have nothing to do with Bobby, whose desk, in the teachers' room, was beside his own. Bobby's desk was at the edge of the English department, and the desk to his left marked the beginning of the physical education department, which had two teachers: Mr. Lee and Miss Lee. Miss Lee was

the only woman on the faculty and Mr. Lee was its youngest man. He was a martial arts expert whose nickname
was Judo Lee, and he seemed intent on becoming Bobby's
friend.

At the far end of the teachers' room was a chalkboard
with room and teaching assignments printed on it. Bobby
could see his name, carefully written at the bottom of the
board, and it was clear that he had the easiest teaching
load. Where the others taught on Saturday mornings, he
was free. Where the others had few breaks during the
day, his schedule showed that he had an easy time of it,
with breaks in the morning and in the afternoon. Mr.
Nam, the English teacher who sat across from him,
seemed offended by his easy schedule. "Look, what an
easy day!" he said, every morning for the first week. He
pointed at the chalkboard and leaned down over Bobby's
desk when he said it, so there was no possibility of mis-
understanding what he meant.

Every morning the faculty of Taechon Boys' Middle
School had a long meeting. Headmaster Kim rarely came,
leaving the vice-headmaster in charge, and the speeches
given by one faculty member or another were long. Bobby
understood little of what went on, so when the bell rang
he was glad to be able to pad in his slippers (all the
teachers checked their shoes at the front door) down the
slick hallways, heading for his first class. His room was
next to Mr. Soh's, and when they walked together Mr.
Soh would often speak kindly to him, recognizing the
difficulty of his adjustment and doing what he could to
relieve it.

When Bobby entered his first class each day the student
monitor would shout and everyone would jump to
attention.

"Good morning, Mr. Bobby," they would say, and he
would then pace about, dividing the room for dialogues

and having them repeat the little dramas from their tired
old books. English, English, English. It was totally useless
to them, one and all.

All the same, the students were wonderful. Bobby was
formal with them, calling them Mr. This and Mr. That
and differentiating between the various Kims and Lees
and Paks by the use of some kind of descriptive adjective:
the handsome Mr. Kim, the baseball-playing Mr. Pak, the
missing-tooth Mr. Lee. When he called on them they
would stand and smile and struggle, putting as much
heart into their English as they had and showboating for
their buddies with as much individualism as they dared.

Each classroom had a round-bellied stove at its center,
but the teachers weren't allowed to light the stoves until
a certain date had passed, and, as of the week after Headmaster Kim's uncle's wife's cousin's funeral, that day still
had not come, though a cold breeze began to insinuate
itself upon the classrooms.

In Bobby's room a rat would occasionally run along the
outside windowsills, causing the students to turn in their
seats and giving Bobby a chance to include the rat in the
sentences he made up. And all he had to do to make the
students laugh was to speak English quickly, leaving them
all behind.

"Now look at that rat, would you?" he would say.
"Maybe we should invite him in for tea," and the students
would roar. At first he thought one or two of them understood, but they did not. They were simply thrilled at the
prospect of watching him break away like that, as if by
such acceleration he could escape back to America where
he, and such breakneck-speed speech, obviously be-
longed.

When the school day ended, the teachers usually left
the campus together, in order to show Headmaster Kim
that there was an esprit de corps that extended even into

their private lives. Some of the teachers had bicycles, so the camaraderie that they exhibited needed only last as far as the walk to the bicycle shed at the edge of the street. Much to his own relief, Mr. Kwak, the third English teacher, was one of these. But for the rest of them, for Mr. Soh and Mr. Nam, for the two physical education Lees and for Bobby, the school day didn't really end until they had walked back into the village proper, where they could turn down their various alleys and be done with each other for a while.

On this day, the Monday after the funeral, Judo Lee spoke just as they came to the edge of the town.

"We need coffee to start the week off right," he said.

Only Mr. Soh and Mr. Nam were still with Bobby and Mr. Lee, and although his comment sounded innocent enough, they both knew that coffee could lead to other things.

"Ah, but it's nearly payday," said Mr. Soh. "Let's go for coffee when we've got some cash."

It so happened that the nearest tearoom was one Bobby had visited over the weekend with the Goma. It was called the Sarang Tabang, the Love Tearoom, and was run by a beautiful young woman named Miss Moon.

"Nonsense," said Mr. Lee. "I've got a tab in there, everything's on me." Since all the teachers had tabs everywhere there was nothing special in Mr. Lee's offer, but now that he had invited them the others could not refuse.

The tearoom was empty, but by the time their eyes adjusted to the dim light, Miss Moon had met them and ushered them to a table in the back. An American song was playing on the tearoom phonograph, and Judo Lee put his arm around Miss Moon and began to sing along:

"I can't say the thing I want to say. . . .
When you're with another man
Da-Da-Da-Da, Answer Yes or No
Darling I will understand. . . ."

Mr. Lee sat down smiling, and Miss Moon put her hand to her mouth, disarmed by his antics.

By the time Miss Moon had brought them their coffee, the four men were warm and smiling at each other like old friends. This is what Bobby wanted, a casual atmosphere in which to make friends. But though two of the men were English teachers, it was Mr. Lee that he wanted most to befriend. Mr. Lee was nearly as big as Bobby, though his weight was proportioned differently, and he had a convivial face. Bobby's Korean had been among the best in his training group and he formed a question for Mr. Lee.

"In America I once tried out for football," he said. "Do you know football?"

"Ah, football," said Mr. Lee.

Bobby didn't want the English teachers to butt in, but Mr. Nam immediately spoke up.

"Mr. Lee is just a baby in English," he said, and though the sentence made no sense, everyone fell silent again.

It is the policy of Korean tearooms to give only little bits of coffee in their cups and Bobby's was gone in an instant, though he knew there were no free refills. During his first visit to the tearoom he had actually asked for a second cup and Miss Moon had looked at him strangely. "But you just had one," she said, and the Goma had nodded hard as if to reassure her that he had. After that the Goma explained to Bobby that coffee was expensive and was meant merely as a kind of ticket to sit. Besides, who really wanted to drink the stuff? Who, among the regular customers, really liked it?

So with Bobby's coffee gone and with their conversation

at a halt, Mr. Lee saw no alternative but to drink up too, and suggest that they repair to the Pusan-chip, his favorite bar, where Mr. Soh had bought the wine for the funeral only a few days before.

The Pusan-chip was at the other end of the town, down by the train station, way past Bobby's inn. The town was dark by the time they left for the bar, but the Goma had seen them and was tagging along. When Bobby saw the Goma he sent him back to the inn for his overcoat. The other teachers, however, didn't acknowledge the Goma's presence, seeming to prefer not to admit his existence at all.

Inside the Pusan-chip sat an old woman and a young one, the owner and the country girl who currently worked for her. Mr. Lee didn't enter singing this time, but the women were clearly glad to see him. No one else was in this place either and the makkoli pots were full.

"Ah, the American," said the older woman. "You've brought the American along."

The Pusan-chip had a dirt floor and a five-stool bar out front. There was also a raised back room with paper doors and a heated floor. The old woman served the makkoli and food, but it was the young woman's job to sit with the customers, to rub her hands across their legs and pour their wine. The young woman's name was Miss Kim, and she was in the back room ahead of them, sitting next to Bobby and making him wonder what she would do.

Before they had really settled themselves, however, the front door opened again and three soldiers came in, rough-looking characters in camouflage uniforms. The soldiers were attached to the U.S. Army, as Mr. Soh had been during the war, but even in uniform they looked like delinquents. They affected a certain insolence in small ways, by a slight swagger and sneer as they walked across the room. When they saw Bobby one of them said, "Oh look, boys' night out."

His English sounded a lot like Mr. Nam's, and Mr. Soh told Mr. Lee to close the door. The soldier who'd spoken, however, thrust his boot up, blocking the way.

Luckily the owner of the bar had the makkoli ready and stood waiting for the soldier to put his foot down so that she could bring it in. She said something Bobby didn't catch, but its meaning was clear enough and the soldier moved away. Mr. Lee took the opportunity to push the paper door shut once the owner was gone.

They had their makkoli and they had Miss Kim, and Bobby wondered if her being there was what had made the soldiers so unfriendly. Mr. Nam was nervous over the encounter, but Mr. Soh and Mr. Lee laughed. "I'm glad my army days are over," said Mr. Soh. "We were always proud. Not like now."

Judo Lee poured the makkoli, and when they were ready to drink the owner came back with a bottle of Specicola for Mr. Nam, who was a Christian and did not drink alcohol. They toasted each other a time or two, but it soon became clear that the evening didn't have the right feel to it. Perhaps the soldiers had spoiled it. Even Mr. Lee would have gone home then, had he been given the chance. Their hostess, Miss Kim, did her best to raise their spirits but she too was giving up when suddenly there was a racket in the other room. Mr. Lee pushed the door open again to reveal one of the KATUSAs wearing Bobby's overcoat and dancing around. Another had the Goma in a headlock, rubbing his ear and making him cry.

Bobby realized what was happening immediately, but feared that since the teachers thought the Goma beneath them, none of them would come to his aid. In fact, Judo Lee at first smiled at the sight. Bobby's overcoat, however, was another matter entirely, and in a moment Mr. Lee and Bobby both stood up, stepping down into the main room at the same time. As Mr. Nam and Mr. Soh moved closer to the door, Miss Kim tried to call Bobby back.

The soldier holding the Goma had rubbed his face so hard that a piece of his scab had come off and his lip was bleeding. Bobby grabbed his free arm and pulled, surprising everybody when his head slipped loose.

"Mr. Bobby," Miss Kim said urgently. The embarrassed soldier took a step in Bobby's direction while the Goma scrambled under a table and came up over by the main door. The other soldier, meanwhile, had taken off the overcoat and let it fall down onto the dirty floor.

"Hey! Hey!" said the owner. "I don't want any fighting in here. Get out! Go outside!"

At that moment, though, everyone focused on Judo Lee. He knelt down gently to pick up the overcoat, brushing the dirt from it as best he could while still crouching. The soldier who'd been advancing on Bobby angled a bit in Mr. Lee's direction and swung his heavy boot back to kick Mr. Lee in the side of the head. The teacher, however, deftly swayed back, just outside of the range of the kick, and then he stood up fast, taking the man's leg with him, using its momentum to help it along its inevitable path toward the ceiling of the room. The man fell down hard, cracking his head on the ground. Mr. Lee looked at the other two soldiers, but they had stopped short, wiping their feet like young bulls, deciding what to do.

"Mr. Lee is an expert in judo," Mr. Nam told the soldiers. "You better go now."

Mr. Lee handed Bobby his coat and then bent down to help the third soldier to his feet, brushing the dirt from him just as he had done from the coat. "No harm done," he told the man. "We are all Koreans and must make a good impression on the outside world." Then he smiled so nicely that the three soldiers smiled back and soon everyone was shaking hands. The Goma came out from his hiding place and Mr. Lee told the owner to charge everyone's makkoli to him.

*   *   *

Before Bobby had really recovered his wits again, it was midnight and he and the Goma were hurrying along the dark street, trying to get back to the inn before the curfew. Judo Lee and the soldiers lived too far from the bar, so they decided to sleep there, all happily moving around the back room in their long underwear. Mr. Soh and Mr. Nam had left a few minutes earlier, and Miss Kim walked with the Goma and Bobby until they got to a certain passageway. Then she too was gone, without so much as a farewell.

Bobby's room was one of the smallest in the inn and the Goma slept in the inn's kitchen, on the dirt floor beside one of the charcoal fires.

"I want to sleep," Bobby said. "I have work tomorrow."

Whenever he spoke to the Goma he used horrible Korean, but the Goma smiled anyway and walked around the inner courtyard with him to the sliding-door entrance of his room.

"Good night, Goma," Bobby said. He pushed the boy back so that he could close his door, but even after the paper partition was between them, the Goma did not move. His shadow swayed on the paper like a burglar's.

Bobby turned on the overhead light and looked about his room. His Peace Corps trunk was closed as he'd left it, a few paperbacks stacked on top. He picked up his little short-wave radio and tried to find the Voice of America, but it was too late for anything but static. When the Goma, still outside the door, cleared his throat, Bobby said, "Go away."

"I will," said the Goma, "but first I have a question." As usual, the Goma was speaking the most rudimentary form of pidgin Korean, the kind he had decided early on was the best way to get through to Bobby.

Bobby opened the door again and looked out into the darkness. "What?" he asked.

"My father is dead and I must return to the countryside for a while," the Goma said.

Bobby understood, but made him repeat it so that he was sure. "Your father's dead?" he asked. "When did you hear? How old was he? How did you find out?"

The Goma smirked in the shadows, but then said that his father had been very old, over eighty. "I don't have any money to go home with," he continued, "nothing with which to buy a bus ticket, nothing to take as a gift."

He was asking for a loan, Bobby realized, but his own salary was a mere thirty-five dollars a month.

"How much do you want?" he asked. "I'm an American, but I'm not rich."

"I need fifteen hundred won," said the Goma.

"Fifteen hundred," Bobby said out loud. About five dollars. "I'll give you a thousand but you have to pay me back."

"Of course," the Goma said.

Bobby took a thousand-won note from his pocket. That left him with three thousand more until the end of the month. But though the Goma had the money, he didn't leave. Something else was on his mind.

"My father was over eighty and I am now eighteen," he said. "I should have a real job by now. I've been working in this inn ever since I was nine."

Bobby looked at the Goma. He had thought that he was no more than about twelve. He was a foot shorter than Bobby and he acted at least six years younger than he was. "What kind of a job would you like then," Bobby asked. "If you're eighteen."

"A real job, a job where you go to work and then come home. A job with a quitting time. I could make more than this every week." He held up the thousand-won note Bobby had given him.

Bobby nodded, about to say more, but he heard a commotion from a room farther down and, not wanting to be a bother to anyone, hurriedly pushed the Goma back, closing the door once more. He turned off his light again and stood there in the dark until the Goma went away.

Bobby unrolled his bedding and lay down diagonally across his room, so that he could stretch his toes and still not touch the wall. He had almost been in a fight that night, saved only by the expert Judo Lee. Perhaps Bobby did not know enough about himself, but he did know that he was not a physical coward. He had had to prove that too many times at home, using his rampant bulk to subdue the muscular insults of those who were always in his way.

He was sleepy and a little sick from the wine, but he was suddenly awake again, gratified by the thought of himself as far better off than the Goma. In America he had a place of his own, at least inside his grandmother's house, but what place did the Goma have? In America Bobby had only his fat and the weakness of his impulses to worry about, but the Goma was pitiful and ugly and decrepit, and the thought of him made Bobby's fatness seem, for a moment, almost beside the point.

As Bobby let the sleep come back, he tried, as an experiment, to imagine the Goma's life instead of his own. He could imagine the Goma quite easily, traveling into the country to bury his father, but he could not imagine what was in the Goma's mind as he went.

I am amazed how fat this American is. He is tall, like all Americans, but he has the shape of a Western pear, with most of its meat down low. I'll wager that he weighs one hundred thirty kilograms, perhaps more. When he got off the train he dwarfed our poor Mr. Soh, but his size, rather than making him seem strong and fit, as is the case with Mr. Lee, gave him a helpless and muddle-headed look. His face is wide and his eyes bulge from it like those of a frog! Also he has poor posture and sits in his chair as if dumped there like a sack of rice. And he makes noise when he walks, which is good, I suppose, because it lets us hear him coming and we can prepare ourselves.

It is odd to have an American in our teachers' room and in our school, but it makes me understand how appropriate our word for foreigner is. The word means "outside person," and all one has to do is observe this man to realize its aptness. He is outside of everything imaginable, and because of it he has no way of relating, no way of being among us, no way of partaking in our everyday lives.

Ah, but this is too complicated for an old country man like myself. Let me be satisfied with the realization that he is "outside," which is so obvious as to be evident to a blind man, and let me not spend so much time thinking about him and worrying about what it all means. Outside is outside, simple as that. It is the opposite of inside, and inside is normalcy, an ordinary view of things. The youngest teacher on our staff could tell me that.

I have decided that I must say something good about this American before I close my diary for the day, and what I have chosen is this: his Korean, though I haven't heard him say much, sounds better than I thought it would, and he is a good singer, who knows all the words to at least one song.

Written as I sit in my study, watching the leaves fall from the plum tree in my neighbor's yard.

4300 年　10 月　20 日

Decrease

*Six in the third place means: When three people
journey together their number decreases by one.*

Bobby was having trouble with an old woman
who hung about the train station and seemed
never to go anywhere else. He'd seen her there on the
night of his arrival, and now whenever he ventured that
way she'd run at him, shout wildly, and try to catch hold
of his arm. The second time he saw her he hadn't been
quick enough and she'd torn his sleeve, so now, whenever he walked that way, he took the Goma along. The
boy didn't hesitate to roll at her knees. He had no mercy
and would hiss like she did whenever the occasion arose.

Though the teachers at school weren't happy about it,
Bobby and the Goma were becoming friends. At least with
the Goma Bobby could be himself, not always on guard,
feeling as though he were on stage. And the fact that the
Goma, like himself, was truly alone in the world made
the friendship seem natural. To be sure, Bobby enjoyed
the idea of having his own sidekick walking the streets
ahead of him, taking the crazy women out of his path,
but it was more than that. Bobby thought of it as a Don

Quixote kind of thing, for though the Goma acted the part of his servant, he continued to speak to Bobby as if he were an idiot, thus reversing what Koreans considered their proper roles to be.

During his first days in Taechon, Bobby hadn't been able to recognize the utter hopelessness of the Korean the Goma used, but as the weeks passed he studied hard, and he improved. Now he found new verbs everywhere, added complex-sentence structure daily, and he had nearly mastered the honorifics, those difficult verb endings that give the Korean language its sliding scale, allowing it to be gross or majestic, belittling or grand, turn and turn about. And all this time the Goma didn't change the way he spoke a whit.

"Hey! You go school?" he would ask every morning. "Hey! Come go tearoom? Hot tea have yes?"

His Korean was bereft of adjectives or prepositions, empty of such easy connectives as "but" or "because," and generally contained nothing but robot directions. Do this. Do that. Go there. Eat this. And the odd thing was that he seemed instantly to have developed this stick-figure language of his upon meeting Bobby. Whenever the Goma was along Bobby could not speak to the real people of the town without him interpreting, shifting the language downward and blurting out obscenities. "Tell me," the town druggist might ask, "have you found adjusting to Korean food difficult? Is our way of life causing you problems?" Before Bobby could absorb the questions and form intelligent answers using the learned Korean in his mind, the Goma would shout his own version into Bobby's ear. "Korean food sticky-sticky? Korean life no good?," and Bobby would somehow be forced to answer with nods and grunts, as if captured by the Goma's way of speech and whisked away from the real thing.

It was infuriating, but it drew Bobby to him nevertheless, and perhaps the reason was this: though the Goma was a bare-bones communicator he did have a way of seeing what the druggist, or anyone else, was really asking, and he translated the suspicion of cultural inferiority implicit in their questions, rather than the words they used.

About six weeks after his arrival in Taechon, Bobby left the village for the first time, heading for a U.S. Army missile base, where he had been invited for Thanksgiving dinner. Thanksgiving had always been a big holiday with Bobby, and he had looked forward to it with what his grandmother justly called gluttony. Now, though, after six weeks of half-ration Korean food, he was beginning to feel a particular looseness in the way his trousers fit, and he rode the train northward in an unusual frame of mind. Would being with Americans again feel strange? Would they once again be repulsed by the way he looked, and would he once again take up the methods he had continually relied upon for getting by, namely facial tricks and a memory for jokes? Though he had been away from Americans for only a short time, he felt a certain tentativeness, and a bewilderment as he realized that he would have been willing to miss the meal.

The train trip was uneventful and Bobby used the time to write a letter to his grandmother and a note to Mrs. Nesbitt, his grandmother's closest friend in the Royal Neighbors lodge, and a woman whose youngest son was missing-in-action in Vietnam. Mrs. Nesbitt had always been kind to Bobby, but the son, Carl, whom he'd known since childhood, had always been a bully and a jerk. Once, at the beach near his house, Carl had seen Bobby in a bathing suit and had actually pushed his fist in among the rolls of Bobby's fat. Bobby had held it there, bending forward and closing himself around Carl's fist and slowly walking toward the water, warding off the blows from Carl's other hand by the simple turning of his head. Bobby's idea was to walk out until Carl's head was below the water level, his own just above. Carl Nesbitt had begged then, and thereafter had hated Bobby completely, though from a distance. Still, Carl and Bobby had been called to their preinduction physicals together, and while Bobby had ballooned to two eighty and was classified unfit, Carl Nesbitt had been healthy and strong, excited to go. It was odd. Bobby had hated Carl all through school, but now he was writing Carl's mother to say how sorry he was.

When the train arrived at the village below the missile base an army truck was waiting, and the private driving it gave Bobby the peace sign as he opened the door. The ride up into the hills took half an hour, and during the trip Bobby lost whatever tentative feelings he'd had on the train. When they parked the truck, the driver, whose name was Ron, told Bobby that the colonel and some other Peace Corps volunteers were waiting in the officers' club, but that if Bobby could spring loose after dinner he should come down to the Vil where Ron had a hooch. "Don't get me wrong," the private said. "The officers here are OK. But later on. You know, when you've had enough."

The officers' club was a flat-roofed, low-built affair, and when Bobby walked in he immediately saw Cherry Consiliak, a black girl from Philadelphia whom he'd furtively ogled during training, and Larry Corsio, a guy he hadn't known at all. They were drinking whiskey and talking to the missile-base officers, a colonel, and three lieutenants, all of them white and smiling.

"Ah, the last arrival," said the colonel. "Bobby, isn't it? Come, let me get you a drink. Pull up a chair."

A table set for seven took up most of the space in the room. Cherry Consiliak, it was easy to see, had decided the predinner configuration by where she sat when she came in. She was a beautiful girl, and though she and Bobby hadn't been close during training, they had often smiled and said hello. Then she had seemed completely out of reach. Now, however, she jumped up and greeted Bobby like a relative.

"Hey!" she said, "God, I've missed you!" She gave him a hug and kissed him across his nose and eyes.

Bobby shook hands with Larry Corsio, and all three of them laughed. It seemed their solitary experiences, over the weeks, had brought them closer together, though they hadn't seen each other at all.

The colonel introduced Bobby to the other officers, and when the introductions were over Cherry and Larry Corsio made room for him between them on the couch.

"This has been the longest six weeks of my life," said Cherry. "Has anyone gone home yet? Has anybody quit?"

Bobby said he didn't know, but Larry said that nobody had. He shook his head and smiled. "We're all going to make it."

Cherry laughed and smiled and held Bobby's hand as if it were he who had voiced such optimism. She leaned up to give him another little kiss, and his heart began to skip around, pounding out a nervous rhythm in his chest. What was going on?

"How much weight have you lost?" Larry asked. "In six weeks I've lost twenty pounds! There is a scale in the colonel's room. Let's go see what it says about you."

Bobby, content on the couch, was completely unprepared for this. He was lighter than he'd been in years—he knew that—but he didn't want to stand up on a scale in front of this girl. His weight had always been an enemy when it came to the women he had liked, and though he had no idea what he weighed now, he didn't want to find out.

But Cherry, whose body seemed perfect to Bobby, smiled and said that she had lost five pounds herself, so Bobby let himself be pulled from the couch.

"We're going in to weigh Bobby," Larry told the colonel, and the officer bowed gallantly, throwing his hand out as if to show them the way.

The colonel's room was small and Larry dragged the scale to the middle of the floor. Before Bobby got on, he took off his shoes and peered at the gauge to make sure that it was set on zero. Cherry was right next to him, so he sighed and stood up on the thing, stealthily trying to cover the needle with his toe.

Larry knelt down. "What did you weigh when you got here?" he asked.

"I don't know," Bobby mumbled, "two fifty, maybe." He knew, of course, that it had been two fifty-five.

Bobby could feel himself growing red, but when Larry pushed his toe out of the way and said, "Two thirty-seven!" he was surprised. And when Larry and Cherry both started laughing, he got down off the scale and joined them, mindlessly happy with the news. He hadn't weighed two thirty-seven since high school.

When they all finally stepped back into the main room the three lieutenants told them that it was time to eat. The lieutenants separated them, as they were no doubt assigned to do, and Bobby was sharply disappointed at seeing Cherry seated so far away. What an easy girl she was to talk to. Why in the world had he not thought so before?

The lieutenant in charge of Bobby was Gary Smith, who was in his twenties and seemed quiet and self-effacing. From Chicago, he had gone to officers' candidate school and said that he'd actually volunteered for Vietnam. "That way I was sure I'd end up somewhere else," he said.

Gary Smith and Bobby sat at the end of the table farthest from Cherry, who was with the colonel at the head. The table was nicely set and despite his weight loss, Bobby was salivating like a dog when the wine came and the colonel raised his glass to propose a toast.

"This is special," he said. "The army is thankful that

these Peace Corps volunteers are with us, and we are thankful that America's presence in Korea is not so totally military as it once was." He raised his glass a little higher. "To Larry, Cherry, and Bobby," he said. "And to peace."

They all said, "To peace," but right after that the turkey came and then the potatoes and the dressing and the rolls, and Bobby forgot everything else. Though he tried for some decorum, he ate like a maniac, hardly stopping to taste his food. The one saving factor was that as he looked down the table he discovered that he was not alone. He was among people now who all ate the American way, finishing everything in less than twenty minutes, with only a little conversation to get in the way.

After dinner there was pumpkin pie, and then the colonel excused himself, saying he was the duty officer but that they could do what they liked, stick around for the movie, stay here and drink, whatever. Bobby saw the colonel touch Cherry's arm before he left. "I've got a fine collection of Motown in my room," he told her. "Feel free to go on in and listen. I'll only be gone a while."

But by the time the colonel closed the door, Cherry was back at Bobby's side and Larry was too. The three of them looked at each other and then sidled up next to Gary Smith.

"Let's walk on down to the Vil for a while," said Larry. "How about we see what's happening in the Vil?"

Gary Smith went to his room and came back wearing his jacket, and the other two lieutenants shook their hands before heading off on their own.

"Who told you about the Vil?" asked Gary. "Did anyone mention me?"

Larry said he hadn't heard anything, and Bobby mentioned Ron's invitation, which had apparently been extended to them all in turn.

"Oh yeah, Ron," said Gary. "He's one of the best guys."

Though Bobby had no clear idea what a "hooch" was, it turned out that Ron and Gary both had hooches in the same low building, on a dirt stretch behind a bar and hidden from view. They walked out of the officers' club, across the missile-base grounds and out the main gate. The Vil seemed made up entirely of bars and tailor shops, each with a certain glossy sheen. In a way it was like being transported back to America and Bobby felt an unexpected little charge. The bar girls standing along the street said hello to Gary and smiled at the rest of them. And when they turned down the pathway Gary showed them, they found Ron standing there waiting, the line of hooches behind him.

"That was fast," said Ron. "The colonel must have gone out early."

"We keep these places as a kind of a getaway," said Gary Smith.

There were six rooms in the building, and Ron and Gary Smith had the last two. It was clear that they were buddies, though that wasn't the impression Gary had given them earlier. And it was interesting to watch Gary change once he shed his responsibilities as an officer on the base. It was like walking down some poor American street with a guy who originally came from there.

Gary's hooch was darkly psychedelic, and as they ducked through the low door Cherry took a firm hold of Bobby's hand. Once they were inside Gary went into the darkest corner and took his uniform completely off. Standing there in his underwear, he slipped into a pair of old jeans and a plain brown T-shirt. There were posters on the walls and pillows all over the floor.

Once they were seated Ron reached over and pushed a button and the place was filled with music, a sweet country-blues tune by Mississippi John Hurt. Soon they had all arranged themselves on the pillows, forming a circle along the edges of the room, and Ron pulled out a noodle package that was stuffed full of marijuana. Bobby had smoked dope only twice before, both times in college, but he was willing to try it again. Cherry, however, surprised them all by speaking up. "I don't know," she said softly, "you guys go ahead. I think I'll pass." She apparently knew the song that Mississippi John Hurt was singing and she took a little of the sting out of her refusal by quickly singing along.

"Got to go to Memphis,
From there to Leland.
Got to see my baby,
'Bout a lovin' spoonful . . ."

Gary rolled a joint, which went by twice. Since Cherry wasn't smoking, Bobby only pretended to, but the room was full of the stuff and he soon began looking at Cherry in a new kind of way. She was a beautiful girl, but what the hell was going on? She hadn't touched him or held his hand in training, so why was she doing it now? Bobby found her refusal to smoke the marijuana wonderful, as if she knew some secret about herself and was avoiding a certain vulnerability, but he didn't understand the rest of it. Perhaps it was only that she, too, had been holed up in a Korean village these past six weeks and was seeking a little release of her own—glad to see him, perhaps, but using him as well.

Still, when Bobby looked at Larry he couldn't help wondering why Cherry wasn't touching him too. He was sitting just as close, after all, on her other side. So if she was glad to see them both, why touch one and not the other, why him and not Larry?

Such questions might have been influenced by the clouds of smoke billowing about the room, but the answer

that Bobby came to was this: though Cherry was glad to
see Larry too, if she were to touch Larry, he would somehow have a right to take her touches in a certain serious
way. Bobby, on the other hand, was a fat boy, and though
he had nearly forgotten it, his role in America, in situations like the one at hand, had always been that of an
asexual friend. Fat girls played that part too. And though
his fluids moved within him just as surely as Larry's did,
Cherry somehow knew that he would not look upon her
touches in the same way that Larry might. Bobby was a
world apart and he was smart. Cherry knew that he would
understand it all and so she touched him and not Larry.
She sighed and kissed him and snuggled close and in
every gesture she knew that he was safe. Goddamn!

The five of them stayed there in Gary's hooch for the
rest of the afternoon, smoking and laughing. It was stupid
and unnecessary, they all said, to go weeks without seeing
each other again. Cherry's village was only a little north
of Larry's and Bobby's was only a little south. Because
the missile base was in the middle, it was the obvious
convenient meeting place, but the Peace Corps volunteers
all urged the G.I.'s to get out and see the real Korea for
a while. So it was decided that Larry and Cherry and
Gary Smith and Ron would all come to Taechon during
Christmas vacation, which was less than a month away.
It'd be great to see each other again. They smiled and
smiled.

After that they spent an hour looking for Ron's truck
keys so that he could drive them down to the station in
time to catch the last train home.

Youthful Folly

━━ ━ ━
━ ━ ━ ━

Nine in the second place means: The son is capable of taking charge of the household.

Nat King Cole was singing "Too Young," and Bobby was watching Miss Moon and remembering the narcotic effect that seeing Cherry Consiliak had had on him when Headmaster Kim came into the Love Tearoom to say that he'd at last found a family with whom Bobby could live.

"They tried to tell us we're too young,
Too young to really be in love . . ."

"Too Young" was Headmaster Kim's favorite song, and he took a moment to listen to it before shaking the winter cold from his coat and sitting down. He had Mr. Soh with him in case Bobby didn't understand.

"I am so relieved," said the headmaster. "You have been staying at the inn too long, my promise unfulfilled."

"It's been fine," Bobby replied, on guard a little. His room at the inn had not been fine, but he wanted to hold on to it until he found out what was in store. Also he was thinking about the Goma. What would happen to him if he moved away?

Though Bobby's Korean was getting better fast, Headmaster Kim insisted on looking at Mr. Soh for a translation. Bobby didn't want to ignore Mr. Soh, but he continued looking directly at the headmaster.

Finally the headmaster said, "Policeman Kim. His house is even closer to school than your inn. I would have asked him earlier but he was in Seoul. There is a boy, a third-year student who is doing poorly in English."

It was very common for Peace Corps volunteers to be taken into someone's home so that they could teach English to members of the family. Some of Bobby's training friends considered this a horrendously self-serving attitude on the part of the Koreans, but Bobby thought it was all right. The rent would be low. He tried to remember his third-year students, but no particular Kim stood out.

"When can I see the place?" he asked.

"Too Young" was going into its third consecutive playing—Miss Moon knew the headmaster's tastes—but rather than answer the question, Headmaster Kim only nodded. "Good," he said. "I will talk to Policeman Kim again and we will go there after school tomorrow. Thank you for your patience at the inn."

He and Mr. Soh stood. It was a Sunday evening and Bobby quickly understood that they had just come from Policeman Kim's and that they were going back there now to make it all final. His seeing the room was the last thing on their minds. And a refusal of it was completely out of the question.

The next day at school, Bobby was surprised to find the teachers not wearing their usual suits but plaid shirts with long boots over their trousers instead. Despite his growing proficiency in Korean he still had little idea of what went on at the morning meetings, so he assumed that he had simply missed an announcement, that this, happily, was a special day of some sort.

It had been two weeks since his return from the missile base, and during that time the weather had grown surprisingly cold. They had reached the date by which the Ministry of Education had decreed heat could be turned on, and the teachers were huddled around the stove, blowing into their hands or warming them on the teacups that they held. Bobby walked up to his friend Mr. Lee and asked, "What's going on?"

Given fresh evidence that no one other than a Korean could ever really speak the language, Mr. Lee found Mr. Kwak and pulled him over to explain.

"Tell him what's happening," he said. "He doesn't understand."

Bobby was glad Mr. Lee hadn't called over Mr. Soh, his usual interpreter. Though Bobby had continued to think of Mr. Kwak as the shy English teacher who immediately left school on his bicycle every day, he somehow liked the older man better than either Mr. Soh or Mr. Nam.

Mr. Kwak grew pensive for a second but then he took off his glasses to clean them on his tie. And, speaking quietly, he said, "You see, once a year we dissolve our regular activities for the day and allow the children to run into the hills to catch rabbits. Today is that day. At the end of the rabbit-catching the teachers will all be made a stew and we will frolic in congeniality, however forced it may appear to be."

Bobby was astounded. Mr. Kwak's English was clear and fluent and easily understood, though he did take his time bringing it out. But it was as if he were showing Bobby some secret part of himself by speaking that way, and immediately Mr. Kwak's stature ballooned, never to be the same again.

"Wow," Bobby said.

Unfortunately Mr. Nam was nearby and came over before Bobby had a chance to say something more clearly expressing his gratitude to Mr. Kwak. Still, Bobby was suddenly sure that he would have two true friends among the teachers: Mr. Kwak and Judo Lee. Judo Lee because of the largeness of his spirit, and Mr. Kwak because he had had the decency and grace to hide the good quality of his English while Bobby was studying Korean. How, Bobby wondered, could he know so clearly, from that frail little statement of his, that Mr. Kwak was at home with himself and someone important in the world?

Policeman Kim did indeed live in a nice house, about halfway between the inn and the school. Policeman Kim was a friend and judo partner of Mr. Lee and it had been Mr. Lee who'd made the initial contact for the school. So after rabbit-catching day and with a full belly of rabbit stew, they all progressed from the inn to Policeman Kim's house.

There were six people in the man's family: his mother, himself, his wife, his two children, and a maid. The middle-school boy who was bad in English was not, it turned out, one of Bobby's students, and the other child went to Taechon Girls' Middle School, which was across town.

When they got to the house Judo Lee opened the door for the Goma, who was struggling along under Bobby's trunk. Headmaster Kim and Mr. Soh were there too, and when Policeman Kim came out Bobby was introduced. He was a broad man of about fifty, who shook Bobby's hand gently, letting him feel the excess flesh of his palm.

"I am rarely home," he said. "But we are glad to have you." He spoke quietly and Bobby could see why he and Mr. Lee were friends. He imagined that their judo matches were full of all kinds of protocol.

Bobby met the children and the grandmother and Policeman Kim's wife, and then everyone took off their shoes and stepped up into the main part of the house to look at Bobby's room. The house was square and contained four rooms and a kitchen. Policeman Kim and his wife shared one room and the grandmother and daughter another. The bad English student was in the smallest room by himself, and Bobby's was the second largest. It had a warm floor and was three times the size of his room at the inn. The Goma brought the trunk in and looked around, his eyes wide but keeping his mouth shut, just as Bobby'd told him he must.

"This is very fine," said Bobby. "I will try not to be a bother."

Policeman Kim chuckled and turned to nod his approval to Judo Lee. Then, as quickly as they had come, everyone left. Bobby had expected that they might all sit around a while, but the day had been long and the cold night was coming in fast. Headmaster Kim kept rubbing his hands together and sighing, clearly happy to be rid of the burden of finding Bobby a home, and Mr. Soh left without having said a word. This time Bobby's Korean had sufficed. Only the Goma hung about the entrance to the house longer than anyone else. "Good-bye, Goma," Bobby said. "We'll be seeing each other soon." He then stepped back into the expansiveness of his new room and closed the door.

Bobby had grown accustomed to the solitude of the inn, for he was surprised when, before he had a chance to organize his things, the grandmother came back in carrying cups on a tray. She was accompanied by the two children. "Let's have some tea!" she shouted. "Maybe I should bring some food!"

Though she was diminutive and old, the grandmother's voice boomed through the house, and when they all sat down, Bobby looked at the children.

"So," he said, "how would you like to learn some English while I'm here?"

The little girl, whose name was Heh Sook, covered her mouth, and the boy turned red, but neither of them spoke.

"Sorry," yelled the grandmother. "They don't speak English!"

"I know," said Bobby. "I wasn't asking whether they spoke English, but whether they'd like to learn."

All of what he had said was in absolutely correct and clear Korean and he was getting irritated. Why was it that no one ever opened their ears when he spoke? Why did they always expect not to understand?

"Not a bit of it!" hollered the grandmother. "Nothing! Not a word!"

This old woman looked hearty enough, but the effort of screaming everything was too much and before she could say anything more, or before Bobby could, she had a coughing fit that simply would not end. She splattered phlegm all about the room, sending armies of germs into Bobby's mouth and lungs. She slumped forward and coughed and coughed. For a few seconds Bobby and the children waited for the fit to stop, but shortly it became clear that they were in for a long wait. Once or twice the grandmother gained slight control over her tremors and put a finger up in the air, but just then the coughing would take over again and away she'd go. Finally Bobby looked at the boy.

"Get her some water, can't you?" he asked.

This time either the boy understood or he got the idea at the same time, for he stood and went quickly back out of the room. The grandmother was coughing on like an old car, and the little girl saw the concern in Bobby's face.

"Do not worry," she said. "She always coughs like this. She's got tuberculosis."

The little girl's face lit up and Bobby looked toward the

side of the room. There were bits of the grandmother's phlegm on his sleeve and the memory of some of it hitting his face came back to him. He moved a little on his cushion, pulling himself up. "Has she seen a doctor?" he asked.

The boy who was bad in English came back in with his father, who was carrying water.

"Here, Mom," he said, "drink up."

The old woman pushed one blind claw into the air, swinging it around until her son caught it and guided it around the glass. He kept hold of it until she gulped a little of the water down. "There, there," he said.

To Bobby's surprise, the water worked a miracle and the coughing stopped. The grandmother's head hung like carrion and Policeman Kim looked at Bobby.

"I think that's enough for tonight," he said softly, and Bobby realized that the man believed his mother had choked on English, that Bobby had started right in teaching her and that the words had gagged her as she tried to bring them up.

"Fine," Bobby said. "Of course." He stood and took one side of the grandmother, with Policeman Kim on the other. "This doesn't happen often," said Policeman Kim. "Only once in a while."

Lifting the woman off the floor, they carried her out of Bobby's room and back into her own. "Ugh," she said. "Ugh, ugh." Once she was safely down again Bobby went back to his own room quickly and closed the door, but in a moment, when he listened, he could hear nothing coming from the old lady's room and he calmed a bit, laughing at the odd sequence of events. The room, after all, was wonderful, the light on the ceiling far brighter than his other light had been. His Peace Corps trunk returned to its normal size in this room, and his books and papers had a desk on which to rest.

Bobby was sleepy and could see his bedding spread

neatly against the nearest wall. It was late and there was school again tomorrow, with real teaching and no more rabbit stew. He took his clothes off and climbed under his heavy quilt. As he was settling himself he began to hear the old grandmother coughing again in the other room. This time, however, she sounded as though she was in control, as though she'd be able to stop herself if this fit of hers went on for too long.

Oppression

$$\equiv\equiv \; \equiv\equiv$$

Six in the third place means: A man permits himself to be oppressed by stone, and leans on thorns and thistles.

It has somehow not become clear yet that Taechon was situated only eight kilometers from a famous beach. There were two Taechons, really—Taechon village and Taechon Beach. The beach, however, like the school heating, had a distinct season, so during the weeks that Bobby had been in town it had not occurred to any of the teachers to take him there. But he had heard of the beach often, and on the weekend before Christmas vacation he decided to go and see it for himself.

It was a rainy Saturday afternoon when Bobby headed out of the house and down past his old inn to the bus stop. He was wearing his heavy overcoat with heavy clothing underneath, and as he passed the inn he pulled his collar up, hoping to avoid the Goma. The inn, however, looked closed, the Goma nowhere in sight. The bus stop was near the train station, so Bobby kept an eye out for the crazy woman as well, but she too was gone. The streets, in fact, were nearly empty. Only a few children were around, coming back from their last Saturday at school before winter vacation, clustered together on the road.

Bobby had the bus to himself and as they wove back through the town he finally did see the Goma, freezing in his threadbare shirt, hopping around the side of the building with a bucket of trash. Soon, however, they were on a road out past the school and into the country, the rice fields shining wet from the side of the road but nobody waving from anywhere for the bus to stop.

There was a kind of town square at the beach, a quirky little turnaround area with a frozen, decrepit fountain at its center. The driver whirled around the fountain, popped the door open and told Bobby to get out fast. "Last bus back is at six o'clock," he said.

As Bobby walked away he buttoned his overcoat again, though the beach felt warmer than the town. And when he finally stopped to get his bearings he realized that this season business was serious stuff. Nothing was open out here, not a hotel or a shop of any kind. He counted six closed hotels, all on the beach side of the street, and all in the kind of faded disrepair that twenty years of summers had caused.

Bobby walked the length of the street and then found a path that cut down to the beach. As he walked on the sand, he watched the wind lifting bits of debris about, the whitecaps as they moved toward shore. This was the Yellow Sea and he was facing China and there was no one, anywhere, but him. This beach did not look very much like the coastline near his grandmother's house, but it did give him the same feeling of loneliness that he'd had at home, and he remembered Carl Nesbitt's fist again, the way he'd sucked it in between his rolls of fat. On that beach he had watched couples stroll, even in winter, arm-in-arm up into the foggy brush.

To Bobby's right the beach seemed quickly to end in

rocks, so he turned left and walked south along the Korean peninsula, imagining as he stepped just where he was in the world and where he ought to be. He was terribly lonely for the first time, but when he tried to think of who he might like to have there with him, no one came to mind. There was only his grandmother; there was Carl Nesbitt, of course. Others had passed through his life quickly, leaving little of themselves for him to hold onto.

Bobby walked to a bend around which he could see nothing but sand and brush and water, no signs of other life at all. He was beginning to feel really cold now, with the new rain needling him and the wind cutting in between the folds of his coat, and he wished he had not let the little bus go back into Taechon alone. Suddenly, though, a voice bleated at him from a spot some distance away. "Baaa," the voice said, and Bobby was reminded of sheep on a hillside, of the springtime countryside on the side of his grandmother's house opposite the beach.

"Baaa! Baaa!"

Though he looked toward where he thought the voice came from, he saw nothing but a bunch of slippery boulders facing the churning sea. He stood still, and in a second one of the boulders stood up, pointed a machine gun at him and spoke again.

"Baaa!"

He had been thinking in English. This was no sheep but a Korean saying, "Hands up."

Bobby raised his hands slowly and on the way put his collar down, exposing his foreign face. The soldier was dressed to melt into the rocky seascape, with seaweed hanging down from his helmet in a strangely feminine way.

And the soldier had seen that Bobby was not Korean, for when he got closer he spoke in English: "Who goes there?"

"It's only me," Bobby answered. "The Peace Corps volunteer from Taechon village."

But speaking in Korean seemed to have been a mistake. The soldier didn't lower his rifle but waved it, up toward the higher ground, telling Bobby to march in front of him. "North Korean spy," he said.

They marched off the beach and through the brush until they came to the gate of a small army compound. Another soldier stood at the gate, and Bobby's captor gave him the first evidence that he wasn't taking things too seriously when he saw the other man. He clowned for the new man a bit, raising and lowering his rifle and sticking out his tongue.

"What do you think, Pak?" he asked the other man. "Is this a North Korean spy?"

Pak didn't understand Bobby's captor's desire to toy with him. "No," he said simply. "He's the Peace Corps volunteer from Taechon village."

Bobby's captor lowered his rifle and gave his friend a disgusted look. "He's not supposed to walk this far down the beach," he said. "What are we going to do?"

He still hoped to throw a scare into Bobby and Bobby was more than willing to go along, but Pak simply said, "Take him down and turn him over to the teacher," and the captor nodded, telling Pak to watch the beach while he was gone.

There were paths all around the army compound and Bobby was told to stay on them, still walking in front of the soldier but noting this time that his rifle was down.

After about five minutes, when his adrenaline had diminished enough for him to be getting cold again, they came to a little clearing where a farmhouse stood. The soldier told Bobby to wait while he went inside. Bobby noticed that the sea was visible again through the trees. They had curved around and come out on the other side of the rocks that the soldier had been guarding. They had now reached higher ground.

The soldier was only gone a moment, but as soon as he left children began to appear, coming around both sides of the house to look. Bobby would have spoken to them, some of whom he recognized from school, but the soldier came out and went back up the path without so much as a farewell. And standing in the doorway, smiling slightly and cleaning his glasses on his tie, stood Mr. Kwak. Bobby still had his hands up, and Mr. Kwak waited until he put them down.

"Taechon Beach is off-limits during the winter season," Mr. Kwak said slowly. "I think there is a sign, but it is written only in Korean."

"I didn't see it. If I had seen it I could have read it," Bobby said.

Mr. Kwak nodded, and then stepped back, inviting him into the house. He had heard the competitive note in Bobby's voice and said, "I would be happy to speak to you only in Korean, if you wish. After all, it is the only way that you can continue to learn."

Though his English was again delivered slowly, it was faultless, and Bobby realized how juvenile he must have sounded.

"I'm sorry," he said. "It's just that among Peace Corps volunteers, ability in Korean is a bone of contention."

Mr. Kwak's English was old-fashioned and deliberate, and when Bobby heard himself speaking, he realized that he was echoing Mr. Kwak's style, playing a role.

They stepped into the main room of Mr. Kwak's house but the children stopped quietly at the door. This room faced the sea and had such a large window that all of the rain and leaves, even the clouds off the bluff, seemed to cling directly to it. It gave Bobby the feeling of being outside but warm.

"This is wonderful," he said. "Have you lived here long?"

There were teacups on the table and Mr. Kwak told one of the children to close the door. "I am not one of the transferrables," he said. "I have always lived here, even when I was a child."

Bobby had recently learned that all teachers were transferred, every six years or so, by the Ministry of Education. Promotions and demotions were subtle affairs, the size and prestige of the school affecting a teacher's sense of himself and, to some extent, his salary.

"How can you be nontransferrable?" he asked. "I thought everyone was."

Mr. Kwak was already sitting down, his back to the howling scene outside. He pushed a cushion around and motioned for Bobby to join him, letting him look, if he would, out at the incredible view.

"Oh, this little farm is my true livelihood," he said. "And sometimes village schools take on a local man."

This didn't seem right, but Bobby didn't want to pry. Mr. Kwak was the best English teacher in the school, and he was the oldest, in his late fifties if Bobby was any kind of judge.

Bobby intended to ask Mr. Kwak how long he'd been teaching at the school, but instead he asked, "How did you learn English so well?"

At this Mr. Kwak passed his hand through the air, disdaining the compliment and chuckling. "Languages are a hobby of mine," he said, "but my English is by no means strong. I am only a dabbler, a language dilettante."

The room was full of books, even the table ladened with them. The books nearest Bobby were in Japanese and the ones by Mr. Kwak were in German. Chinese books lined the bottom of his window. The more Bobby looked the more he saw: Latin, then Greek. There were titles along some of the bindings in languages that Bobby couldn't recognize. Mr. Kwak saw him looking and waved his hand again, as if to apologize for the erudite nature of the room.

"My wife accuses me of studying a new language every time we have a child," he said. "It is an obsession and I'm afraid I am not a very good father because of it."

Bobby asked the obvious question. "How many children do you have?"

"We have nine," said Mr. Kwak, "but please, it was not my intention to brag."

Bobby picked up a teacup and was quiet for a while, letting everything sink in. He was proud of his ability in Korean, but was busy studying it at least in part so that he could better his fellow Peace Corps volunteers when the time came. Mr. Kwak, on the other hand, was studying for the joy of it and Bobby felt himself wake up. He looked at Mr. Kwak and said, "It is wonderful to be here with you. I have been so lonely."

When he spoke, his heart was in his throat and he nearly sobbed. And he was so embarrassed by his words that he had to look away. Powers were at work here that Bobby didn't understand at all. Mr. Kwak, meanwhile, began cleaning his glasses again. Luckily one of Mr. Kwak's children opened the door just then, and came in to sit upon his father's lap.

"Ah," said Mr. Kwak, letting them both focus on the boy. "This is Bo Peep, my youngest. He is only five years old but he is the true intellectual of the family."

Bobby was in emotional turmoil, perhaps, but surely Mr. Kwak could not have said Bo Peep. The boy's black hair stood straight up from his head like he'd recently received a terrible scare. He was a goofy-looking little kid, and when he smiled up at his father Bobby saw a strong resemblance.

"Bo Peep," said Mr. Kwak, still speaking English, "this is Mr. Comstock. He teaches with me at the school."

"Ah," said Bo Peep. "How do you do?"

Bobby looked around the room. This was some kind of trick—the Kwak family ventriloquist was hiding somewhere behind a stack of books. He grinned, trying to catch the boy up. "What's my name?" he asked.

Bo Peep looked stumped and Bobby immediately felt guilty. But then the boy looked up at his father. "What was it, Daddy?" he asked.

"Mr. Comstock," said Mr. Kwak.

"Mr. Comstock," said Bo Peep.

Bobby was stunned. Though the boy was five years old he looked even younger. "You can call me Bobby," he said, and he drank the rest of his tea, which had gone cold and chilled him all the way down.

Bobby stayed at Mr. Kwak's house for a few more hours, until a break in the weather let him hurry down the pathway to catch the six o'clock bus back to town. He was feeling fine after meeting Mr. Kwak and his son. They had talked about ideas, about differences and similarities, about one country and another, and about language, of course. And though Bobby could not have said precisely why, he was feeling, as he left, that loneliness was as elusive a concept as love, and as difficult to focus upon.

Such thoughts preoccupied him until he got to Taechon village. He had walked halfway back to Policeman Kim's house, nearly past his old inn when a familiar braying brought Bobby back to himself. The Goma ran from the doorway to greet him.

"Oi," he said. "Drink tea go?"

"What about the money you owe me?" Bobby asked gruffly. "What about my thousand won?"

The Goma pulled at Bobby's sleeve and grinned. His lip was bleeding again where someone had whacked him, knocking the scab away.

When they got to the Love Tearoom, Miss Moon, in her formal Korean dress, hurried over to meet them. "Your friends were here," she said nicely. "A Negro girl and two American soldiers." She put her hand on Bobby's arm and smiled, but the thought of missing Cherry Consiliak turned Bobby's mood dark again.

Still, he stood there for a time, trying to remember the nature of Cherry's interest in him, still strongly possessed by whatever he had learned from Mr. Kwak, touching Miss Moon and letting the Goma decide what it was that he wanted to drink.

How cold it is this season and how stark the mountains look as I bicycle my way back home in the moonlight after a long day at school.

It is strange to understand that one spends more time thinking about the nature of life as one approaches the end of it. I have kept my journals for forty years—there are stacks of them in my closet—and when I read the earlier ones, it startles me to see the man I was. Of course I have always had this philosophical bent, but those early journals contain entries that appear to me now to be shallow and mundane. In one journal, for example, I wrote the name of a particular wine-house girl seven times. Seven times this woman's name is in my journal, yet now I remember her not. Who was this girl? Is she now dead? Or if she is alive, do her wrinkles reminisce, remembering the fullness of the beauty they once contained?

We do, I think, end our lives as we have led them. The Christians believe that one can turn things around even on one's deathbed, but I don't agree with that. The lead we write with is a part of the pencil, that's what I believe. . . . We are what is written. I, for example, had I my life to live over again, would surely not live it very differently. I have three sons and two daughters; how many men can say that? And two of my sons have three sons as well, and both of my daughters have married above them and have borne sons for the families of their husbands. These are concrete ways of judging a life, and as I notice a progressive brittleness in my bones, I progressively value the concrete.

Lately I have been grumbling on about the American, blaming him actually. I know that is unfair, and I am going to stop it. After all, he is only one, odd-looking man, and I know that I have been short with him because it strikes me that the example he sets is wrong. He has no decorum with the students, no bearing. And he is too friendly. He is a teacher, yet the other day I saw him walking along the street with a beggar by his side. He and the beggar were laughing—braying is a better word for it—and when the American leaned his enormous head back to share in a guffaw, I could see an uncomfortable and frightening new world down the huge channel of his throat as I quickly passed by.

But I do not dislike the American. As a matter of fact, though I distrust what he represents, I am interested in him, drawn to him oddly, like a hand to an uncomfortable bruise.

Written on a cold Sunday morning, in the Pleasant Feeling Tearoom, as I wait for Mr. Song to arrive for our *paduk* game.

4300 年　12 月　24 日

Limitation

Six in the third place means: He who knows no limitation will have cause to lament.

Bobby had been at peace with himself when he'd come back to town, but by the time he left the tearoom the thought of missing Cherry Consiliak had ruined all of that. To be sure, they had planned to meet during winter vacation, but Bobby had not understood that it would be today, when school had just gotten out. He remembered distinctly, in fact, that it had been tomorrow, or perhaps the day after. . . .

Once outside the tearoom Bobby turned toward the Goma and spoke harshly. "Did you see my friends too, the ones who came to town?"

The Goma gave a little shrug and held up a piece of paper, trying to unfold it with his filthy hands.

"What is it?" said Bobby. "Give it here."

The paper was a note from Cherry, which had been tucked beneath the Goma's belt. She had looked for him at the inn and at the various tearooms around town, and she would be waiting at the train station until the last train left for Seoul. "If I don't see you, have a wonderful Christmas," the note concluded. "I had hoped we'd be able to see each other one more time."

Bobby looked at the Goma and felt like smashing him. What a little unreliable jerk! Why hadn't he given him the note before?

"What time is it?" Bobby demanded.

The Goma shrugged again and then Bobby did shove him. "When is the last train to Seoul?" he shouted.

"One go early, one go late," said the Goma.

From the inn Bobby could have walked to the station in five minutes, but from where they stood it would take ten. He gave the Goma another push and took off quickly, his coat flapping in the breeze as he ran. He could feel his flesh bouncing arhythmically, and as he looked to his side he saw the Goma darting along, but he didn't pause to consider how absurd he must look, and he did not slow down. At the station even the crazy woman stood clear when she saw the speed he'd built up. He vaulted the turnstile, making the train man blink, and stopped only when he was about to be pitched down onto the empty tracks.

"Where's the train to Seoul?" he asked when the train man came tentatively up to his side. The Goma had stopped short of this last, law-breaking activity and was waiting in the station proper, gasping for breath.

"Gone," said the man. "Twenty minutes ago. Nothing more until the local at midnight."

Accompanying Bobby's feeling of despair was a physical illness of a sort. He had not only sprinted through the town, but he had jumped the turnstile, pushing his heavy body up into the air, and now he was paying the price. He held his heart and put his other hand upon the train man's shoulder. Where was his dignity, where was his recently secured peace of mind?

Bobby tried to concentrate, hoping to God he wouldn't

throw up, but the station man smiled. "Never mind," he said. "The evening air is fresh and there are the others. . . . I believe they are waiting for you in the truck."

"What?"

"Those who brought the young lady. They are your acquaintances also, are they not?"

This station man was old and his face was friendly. "Such a big truck," he said. "They are letting it idle while they decide what they want to do."

Bobby straightened up, letting Cherry go and feeling his nausea subside. He peered back through the station waiting room, and sure enough, the fender of a big army truck was in plain view, parked out on the narrow street right in front.

The station man laughed and brought some water over from a nearby tap. He helped Bobby wash his forehead and push the worst of his hair from his eyes. When Bobby went back into the station the Goma pressed his body against the wall, rolling his eyes in a bad imitation of terror. Soon, however, he fell in behind.

Now that he was walking, this truck seemed impossible to have missed. Ron and Gary Smith were sitting in it and waved when they saw Bobby coming. Though he had flashed by like a meteor, they didn't seem to have caught any sense of his mood.

"Man, you can run," said Ron. "We thought we'd just wait out here rather than try to catch you."

"Hey!" said Bobby. "Great to see you guys."

He was smiling like a fool, his face round and wet, his voice too loud. Slow down, he told himself, stop your manic ways.

Ron was driving and Gary was sitting there with a beer in his hand. They were both dressed in army fatigues and Bobby realized, as the truck doors opened, that it really was good to see them—far better, anyway, than spending the night alone.

"I didn't know it was today," he said. "I mean, did we set today as the day you'd come?"

"No, it was Cherry," said Gary. "She's going to Japan and wanted to see you to explain her change of plans."

When Bobby heard this he was suddenly sure that she was quitting. Cherry Consiliak was going home. When he asked about it, though, Ron said she was on vacation, that she was meeting someone in Seoul.

All the Peace Corps volunteers were on vacation now that school was out, but it hadn't occurred to Bobby to leave the country. Christ, he thought, they'd only been here since October. What was she going to use for money?

"Listen," he said, "how long can you guys stay? I can't put you up but there's an inn. . . ."

Ron looked up at the truck and Gary shook his head. "We're pushing things real hard now," he said. "We're on duty. Got to get this truck back by morning."

They were near the Pusan-chip, which didn't serve beer, but Bobby got the idea that these guys might like to try some makkoli. The missile base, surely, was no more than a two-hour drive.

"My hometown bar is right here," he said. "Come on. Let's get drunk."

Gary and Ron went around and hopped up into the back of the truck, and while he waited, Bobby turned to look at the Goma, whom he could feel standing near him. It wasn't the Goma, though, but the crazy woman, and she held out her hand, calmly advancing toward him.

"Give me some money or I'll bite you," she said. Was this what she had been saying all along? She curled her lips back and advanced strategically, but though she garbled her words just as she always had, they were suddenly clear. No reason for any trouble, just pay up. Bobby reached into his pocket and found a rumpled note, and when he held it up she closed her mouth, surprised.

"Sorry," he said. "I didn't understand before."

Ron and Gary jumped down from the truck then, so the woman took the note quickly and moved aside. They had gone into the truck to change their clothes and were wearing jeans and sweaters now beneath their regulation army coats.

Bobby had never known the Pusan-chip to be very crowded, but tonight it was full. The back room held a group of six, and there were only three stools left out front. He looked at Ron and Gary to see how the place suited them, but they seemed fine, so he pulled the stools around and they all sat down. The Goma had come in too and was huddled over by the door.

"Ah, teacher," said the owner. "Welcome." The other customers had grown quiet, but because of the owner's friendliness they soon started talking again. Miss Kim was sitting with the group in the back room, and she looked at Bobby and waved. The owner, in the meantime, had brought a pot of makkoli and was staring at the soldiers.

"This is the best makkoli available," she said. She then waited until Bobby had translated for his friends.

Bobby was sitting between the two others, and he quickly raised his bowl, draining it all. Ron and Gary hadn't touched their drinks yet, so he flicked the residue from his bowl and offered it to Ron, Korean-style.

"This is what they do here," he said. "Now you've got to drink everything."

Ron did what Bobby told him, and then he and Bobby both ganged up on Gary Smith. They hadn't been there five minutes when the owner brought another pot.

The Pusan-chip was full of farmers and day laborers from the railroad, men who had been laying another spur out from town, working along in front of a steam locomotive. The laborers were sitting closeby and the farmers were in the back room. After some discussion the laborers bought the Americans a pot of makkoli, and when the owner brought it over, all the laborers bowed. The farmers leaned out to see what was going on.

"Thanks," said Bobby. "Great. Thank you very much."

He and Ron and Gary bowed to the laborers, and in a minute Bobby had the owner send a pot back to them, and one to the farmers as well. The farmers then sent a pot out to the Americans and, for good measure and because they'd come late to the thing, they sent a pot to the laborers, who were happy to have come out ahead. And in order to confuse things even more, one of the farmers got down and carried a full makkoli pot around the room, filling everyone's bowl.

"This is great," said Gary. "In the Vil people are always suspicious. There are never any guys like these hanging around."

Bobby swept his arm around the room. "This is a great village and these are all great men," he said.

Ron and Gary quickly agreed, and suddenly Ron grabbed Bobby's arm. "They *are* great men," he said. "Tell them so, would you? Stand up right now and tell them that they're all great men."

Ron seemed so taken with the thought that Bobby stood and attempted to get everyone's attention by rapping his knuckle against the edge of his bowl.

"Hey," said one of the laborers. "Hey, look at that."

"My friends and I want you to know that we think Taechon is a great village," Bobby said. "And we think its people are great too." He wanted to say that the people in the village were what made it great, but he didn't know how.

The farmers and laborers sat there staring.

"What else?" Bobby asked, looking at Gary and Ron.

"Tell them we think Korea is better than Vietnam," Gary said, and Ron chimed in, "Tell them the whole evening is on us. All the drinking."

But Bobby had paused too long and the others, believing that he was finished, began to applaud. And after that one member from each group stood to answer his praise with drunken praise of his own. Both men stood at the same instant and then each tried to relinquish the floor.

Finally the farmer stood alone, weaving back and forth, his toes hooked over the edge of the upper-room floor. "This is really something," he said. "In all our years coming here to drink we've never had such an experience as this." He looked back at his contingency and they all nodded. "Always before we have seen Americans in trucks," he said, "but you are real people, not in trucks." For a moment the farmer stopped like Bobby had, utterly taken with the thought that they were all real people, and when the laborer edged up off his stool again, the farmer saw him and sat back down quickly, giving up the floor.

"I'm only a laborer," said the man, "and don't know as much as a farmer, but I want to tell you something that I remember. When I was a young man, an American soldier saved my life. I was running from the North Koreans and the American soldier picked me up on his motorcycle, letting me ride to safety on the back of it, my arms wrapped around his middle. His name was Daryl Prescott and I only wondered if any of you know him, where he might be today."

His pronunciation of the name Daryl Prescott was so clear, so well practiced, that Ron and Gary both heard it coming from an otherwise indivisible wave of sound.

"Who the hell is Daryl Prescott?" asked Gary, and the laborer said, "Right, have you seen him? Do you know where he might be today?"

The evening got a little hard to remember after that. The owner was drawn into the drinking, and soon Miss Kim came down to sit upon Bobby's knee, ordered to do so by one of the farmers. The farmers and the laborers had mixed their groups, and the laborer who knew Daryl Prescott tried sitting with the three Americans for a while, but since they had nothing to say about Daryl, he soon moved his stool away again.

And for the rest of the night they drank and drank. Ron wanted Bobby to help him flirt with Miss Kim, but Bobby instead used everything to his own advantage. Ron saw it and began looking down. "God, I wish I spoke Korean," he said over and over again. Then Bobby told Miss Kim that Ron was in love with her and she changed laps for a while, exchanging little glances with Ron and making him smile.

Bobby had been talking to Gary a few minutes when Gary said, "I've been down to her village twice." It took Bobby a moment to realize that he was talking about Cherry. Were his feelings so obvious, then? Had Gary, after all, seen the desperation in his run?

"Who's she going to Japan with?" Bobby asked. "Is it another woman? I know them all."

Gary shrugged. "I don't know," he said, and suddenly it was clear to Bobby that Gary hadn't intuited anything, but was only looking for someone on whom to unburden himself. He was interested in Cherry too!

Bobby turned a frowning face in Gary's direction. "Since she's not here, why talk about her?" he said, and the drink was spinning so wildly in his head that he had to close his mouth to keep more words from coming out.

Luckily the Goma got into some trouble then, closing the door on the subject of Cherry Consiliak. The Goma had been sitting in the doorway, and one of the laborers had kicked at him when trying to go outside. It wasn't much, but the Goma howled so loudly that the owner told him he'd have to leave.

"Maybe it's time for us to go too," said Gary, touching Ron's sleeve. "It's late."

"Oh Christ," said Ron. He and Miss Kim had been

quiet for a long time now, but were still sitting together.

"Really," said Gary. "Look, it's eleven thirty."

Bobby didn't think it could be, but Gary's watch said so. Curfew was in half an hour. Bobby knew, however, that the army was exempt from it.

"Everybody's going home soon," he said.

Ron sighed and dislodged Miss Kim, who stood up easily, soberer than anybody else. "Righto," said Ron.

Miss Kim went back to the farmers, but by then everyone was up, getting ready to go. The owner gave Bobby another chit to sign, more to be added to his steadily growing tab, and suddenly they were all out the door together, into the absolutely freezing night. "Good-bye! Good-bye!"

When they got to the truck everyone was so drunk that nothing mattered. Ron managed to unlock the door and start the engine in what appeared to be a single motion, and once Gary was on board the truck lurched away. There was no time for last-minute comments. The truck was the drunk now and everybody moved to stay out of its way.

God it's cold, Bobby thought, looking up at the high moon and stars. It was so cold that a man could die, lying down in the street like Bobby wanted to do. At least he had his coat. The Goma was in shirtsleeves, wearing almost nothing by his side. "Go home," Bobby told him. "Hurry."

Bobby walked past the Pusan-chip again to catch the opposite road to Policeman Kim's house, and when he looked back he saw the Goma coming his way.

"No!" he shouted. Then he reached down and found a rock to throw, missing the Goma by a mile but making him run.

When Bobby was halfway home the curfew whistle blew, chilling him to the bone. And though he tried his best, he could not stop staggering. There was nobody else on the road, no sign of the laborers or farmers, and when he passed the police station it too seemed dead. Only when he got to the far edge of the village, did he see a tiny light on in the tearoom. "Ah ha," he mumbled. He staggered that way, weaving like crazy but laying a quiet knock on the door.

"Who is it?" said Miss Moon.

"It's me, late and drunk."

Bobby didn't think she would let him in, but she opened the door readily, letting him pass into the tearoom's warmth, its stove still hot, its music still lightly playing.

"My," said Miss Moon. "You're a mess."

Bobby smiled, and when he took her in his arms she didn't seem startled and didn't move away.

She let Bobby kiss her cheek and hold her for a moment before turning him back toward the door. "Sometime perhaps," she said. "But not tonight."

Once outside again Bobby got home in no time without falling or disgracing himself further on the lonely road. No one was up when he entered the house, and there was no sound, not even that of the grandmother's cough. In his room he climbed under his blankets and turned his radio on, letting the static sing to him, letting it buzz around the room as he passed out, the soles of both feet planted firmly on the floor.

The Arousing

Nine in the beginning means: Shock comes—
Oh, Oh!

Bobby awoke at dawn, as the hostile winter-morning light settled about the corners of his room. His first thought was: if I move I will die. He was breathing and his eyes were slits to see through, but the room looked dead and he got the feeling that he'd been transported out of the world into a hospital ward in hell, where there were beds but no medications, diseases but no cures for them at all.

He was still, in a way, wearing his clothes. That is, his overcoat was on, but his pants were down around his knees. He could see his shoes pointing up at the bottom of his blanket, like the feet of some long, cloven beast, and at the sight of them he uttered a silent cry. No one wore shoes in the house. What if he'd marked the floor, what if there were mud smudges leading to his door?

Ah, but if Bobby had had only the telltale smudges of muddy shoes to live with how good life would have been. He turned then, only a little, to test his ability to do so, and he came face to face with a monster. Lying there on the floor beside him, a foot from his head, was a sculpture of something awful, the evidence no lawyer would take into court. Was it the brains of a cow slain in some midnight satanic ritual? Was it a part of his own stomach, dislodged from his body in a fit of alcoholic wretching? No, it was simply this: a pile of excrement half the size of his head, laid there by himself when he'd dropped his pants sometime during the night.

Think of it—he had shit in his room. Bobby lay eye to eye with it for a moment and then opened his nose, testing, to see if its smell permeated the whole of Policeman Kim's house. He was a disgrace, a bum, the lowest example of what a good-intentioned man could become, and he pictured the newspaper headlines in his hometown: "BOBBY COMSTOCK SHITS IN ROOM, DISCHARGED FROM PEACE CORPS." Oh, it was awful! But for some reason, perhaps because he was made of the same stuff, he couldn't smell it.

Bobby got up quietly and looked around for a tool of some kind, something he could use as a shovel. There was nothing much. There were books, but what writer's work could he put to such use? There was his Peace Corps trunk with his clothing in it and on top of the trunk were the letters he had gotten. Finally he spotted a stack of clean Korean aerograms, the ones he intended to use to answer the letters he had received.

Bobby took the stack of aerograms and, picking up a ruler that lay beside them, approached his disgraceful mound. He sat down and pushed as much excrement onto each aerogram as he thought it would hold. For a moment he considered sealing the aerograms, but abandoned the idea. Of the dozen aerograms, he used ten of them to carry his awful message of disrespect away. He had to make two trips to the outhouse, five aerograms piled high in his hands each trip, and then he threw the ruler down into the pit after them for good measure.

On his way back to the house Bobby removed his T-shirt and soaked it in a bucket of freezing water. The morning was as cold as the night before had been, and when he returned to his room to scrub the spot away, he was shivering uncontrollably. He managed to wipe the T-shirt several times across the floor, and then he threw it out the window and crawled back into bed just a second before the grandmother pushed his door open and came in to see what was going on.

"*Aigo*," she said. "You've been farting. I could smell it all the way to my room."

Bobby tried to answer but could only shiver. He'd placed a woven basket on the spot where the shit had been and had scooted his bedding closer to it to discourage anyone from standing just there.

The grandmother peered at him closely. "Are you merely hung over," she asked, "or are you really ill?"

Again, though he tried to answer, to say that it was just the wine, when he opened his mouth his teeth banged together like knives on a chopping block.

"Phew!" she said. "I better call the doctor. Something else is wrong here." She got another two quilts and laid them over him gently, and then she went out the door. It was still barely six in the morning, and it was Sunday so Bobby knew she'd be back alone. Who could she find now, at this hour of the day?

But in truth he did feel worse than he had ever felt before, and he was beginning to believe that it was more than just the wine and his shame. His bowels started to grumble, and he felt the need to get up and go back to the outhouse, but he was shivering so violently that he could not easily move. And soon a sharp pain came across the lowest part of his abdomen, like screws winding remorselessly in.

"Ohhh," Bobby moaned, and the boy who was bad in

English stuck his head through the door. Why could he never remember this boy's name?

"Outhouse go?" he asked.

"Please," said Bobby. "If you could give me a hand."

The boy came cheerfully into the room, somehow getting Bobby to his feet quite easily, wrapping his overcoat around him before lugging him out the door. He was a strong boy for one so small, but Bobby's feet were moving too, though he felt an ache all along his legs when he put his weight on them. How in the world had he found the strength to carry the aerograms out the way he had?

When they got to the outhouse the boy left Bobby alone, walking a short distance away. Inside the dismal shack Bobby looked down through the thin floorboards at the various triangles of blue there on that hard brown sea. He was shaking so much that he had trouble bending his knees, and once he was squatted there, hands against the walls, he was sure his weight would break the boards and that he would tumble down there himself, to die among his ten messages.

As he emptied his bowels and covered the evidence, however, the vise in Bobby's belly loosened and he was able to stand and open the door, walking back to his room alone.

Bobby wanted nothing but the warmth of his blankets and the quiet of an entire day to sleep, but when he entered his room again the grandmother was there. She was alone, but she had a shawl full of medicines and herbs, and when Bobby passed her, dropping his overcoat and climbing back into bed, she knelt down at his side.

"Open your mouth," she said. Bobby's shivering had continued full force, though, and he could only open it and close it intermittently, like a dying fish.

The grandmother unfolded her bundle and removed from it a silver cutting knife and the still bloody antler of a reindeer. Seeing the stub of the deer's horn made Bobby sicker and he said, "No, I'm not taking that. It is against the Peace Corps rules. I can only take American medicine."

He spoke emphatically, but the grandmother continued scraping the bloody end of the antler and mixing what she got there with the powders she'd taken from another canister. When she had the medicine ready she looked at Bobby and he summoned all his energy to shout: "No! Go on now! Get out of here!"

He used a guttural form of language and his rudeness had connected this time. The grandmother looked appalled and immediately packed everything up and hurried from the room. Bobby really was sick, for with the old lady gone he fell away from all his troubles in an instant and dreamed of being a child at play, at his own grandmother's house.

But when he woke it was not, yet, because of his need to return to the outhouse. He had started dreaming of a dust storm, of walking unprotected among the whirling sands, when suddenly he began to cough and sputter and spit. He sat up in bed and when he opened his eyes again he saw that the grandmother was back, a roguish smile spread across her face. In one hand she held the empty vial that had contained the reindeer-antler potion that she'd made, and in the other a funnel formed from Bobby's last two aerograms, a funnel that she'd just removed from his wide-open mouth.

Bobby ended the year like that, much of his holiday taken up with the dysentery or flu or whatever it was. The grandmother came often and he no longer fought her visits and he took whatever it was she gave him.

She told stories of how it had been in the old days, and Heh Sook and the boy who was bad in English came in to tuck their feet beneath the blankets and listen.

When it came time to go back to school Bobby was well again, but for a long while his defenses had been so low that the grandmother's tuberculosis germs took the opportunity and moved from the walls of his esophagus into the softer tissue of his lungs where they multiplied.

The American has been here for months now and I was worrying about the fact that I had still not spoken to him, worrying whether he had noticed and whether he thought my silence an unkindness of some kind, when he walked up and spoke directly to me. I was astonished. He spoke in Korean, and though his words were strange, I understood them. He was asking me if I would like to join an evening English class that he had organized for the benefit of the teachers of the school.

I was so taken aback that my mouth hung open like a stupid old bird's. I said, "I have enough trouble with Korean," an expression that made the American smile, and one in which I have taken some pride now that I've had time to think it over. "I have enough trouble with Korean." Considering that I did not expect him to come to my desk and that I had no time to prepare what I would say, I think such a statement exhibits my good training pretty well. It is disarming, it is self-effacing, and it is polite. All in all, it is a very good thing to say, and I have learned from it the lesson that spontaneity is not always bad.

The truth of the matter is that I have been wanting to speak to the American, but I have been muddling around, imagining myself walking up to him and delivering some comment like, "Good day, sir," which any fool knows will almost always bring the response of "Good day." I might have said something about the business of the school, of course, but I was afraid anything like that would be too complicated and he would not understand. How wonderful, then, that it is all cleared up now. "I have enough trouble with Korean!" Not bad at all.

I have noticed that my fascination with this American is not so far removed from the fascination one feels during a courtship, and that makes me pause and chuckle. How is it that I have become so enamored with the man? It is as if the Chinese circus has come to town and I am spending all my money to stand inside its strangest tent.

Written on the slow train to Hongsong, as I work my way up the coast to see my younger brother.

4301 年　3 月　9 日

Part Two

Retreat

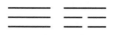

Nine in the fourth place means: Voluntary retreat brings good fortune to the superior man.

At the back of the school there was a big room housing the library, and Mr. Soh, once a week, was the school librarian. There weren't many books in the library, but it had the school's best stove, and for that reason Mr. Soh had reserved it for Bobby's special English class, the one he had been promising to teach ever since his arrival in town.

By now Bobby understood, of course, that teaching in Taechon Boys' Middle School was a worthless occupation for a Peace Corps volunteer—even his best students would end their formal education after ninth grade. He had been assigned there, he had come to realize, simply because the Ministry of Education had been given the job of placing the Peace Corps volunteers and had not known what to do. He was a commodity, a badge of improvement for the community, and nothing more.

But if he was going to make the best of it, he asked himself, why not teach a special class for teachers and adults, since there were some who were interested? Headmaster Kim, when he heard about it, wanted to charge the teachers and pay Bobby extra for his work but Bobby said no. His only other stipulation was that they not go drinking after class. He was healthy again, and he wanted to stay that way.

The first students to enroll in the special class were Mr. Soh, Mr. Kwak, and Mr. Nam. Bobby hadn't intended that the class be exclusively for teachers at the school, but since it was on school property and a considerable walk from town, no one else joined. Finally, though, Judo Lee and Miss Lee signed up. Bobby asked the headmaster and vice-headmaster if they too would like to join the class but they both declined. "English is the language of the young," said Headmaster Kim. "I have enough trouble with Korean," said his assistant.

On the first night of class, Mr. Soh went back to school early to relight the library fire, and the rest of them followed later on. When Bobby left his room, walking up the pathway leading to the main road, he envisioned himself not so much as a teacher but as a leader of discussions, keeping everything simple but letting the others do most of the talking. He wanted this to be something he did well. His students would learn that the English language, too, was flexible and could be used creatively by someone with control. Never mind that the students were of vastly different abilities; he would trim his lesson to include them all.

Bobby was walking quickly, looking at the moon and thinking over the potential difficulties of the class, when the Goma appeared from the shadows, underdressed as usual and ignoring the cold night. Though Bobby had been living with Policeman Kim for several months, he had continued meeting the Goma occasionally, so seeing him pop up wasn't surprising. There was no place for him among the teachers, however, and Bobby told him so.

"Teach me too," said the Goma. "Big-time class start right now."

The more Korean Bobby learned, the more atrocious the Goma's became. "No, Goma," he said. "This class is for the teachers, not for you."

"Please," the Goma said quietly. "It is my only chance."

Bobby stared at him. His only chance for what? He couldn't speak Korean well, he had never been to school, and the teachers would surely be insulted by his presence in the room. Still, he had spoken very well just then, and Bobby knew all too clearly what being an outcast was like. Did the Goma really think he had some kind of chance? He didn't even have a winter coat, let alone any kind of chance.

"Please," the Goma said, seeing something like real consideration in Bobby's eyes. "If I learn English I can go to America, be your boy. Or I can hang out with army, get lost, find my way."

Bobby looked at him. "The teachers won't like it," he said, and at the same time he realized that he was going to take the boy along.

"Screw the teachers," said the Goma, reverting to pidgin again and making Bobby wince. What was he getting himself into?

When they entered the library, the others had already arrived. The stove was hot and a pot of barley tea was steaming on top of it. Bobby tried to make light of the Goma's presence, but even Mr. Kwak seemed surprised by it. "He's only here to listen," Bobby said in English. "Think of it as our good deed." And the Goma, as if concurring, scurried into the corner, making himself small.

Bobby sat in a chair that the teachers had placed at the head of the table, closest to the stove. Mr. Lee and Miss

Lee were beside him, and Mr. Soh was at the far end
with Mr. Kwak and Mr. Nam.

"All right," Bobby said. "Let's try this. Let's speak only
English, or let's try to anyway. Let's not use Korean except
for clarification."

Bobby said this twice, first in English, then in Korean,
and everyone nodded, faces expectant and bright.

Bobby had a notebook with him, but all he'd managed
to prepare was a list of possible discussion topics: the
upcoming U.S. election, popular music around the world,
Korean-American relations, the recent defection to the
South of a North Korean big shot. He was about to suggest
that they start with something simple when Mr. Nam
stood up and began walking around the table, passing
out books. "Here we go," he said.

Bobby wanted to object, but Mr. Nam astonished him
by handing a book to the Goma, who was still slumped
against a bookcase at the rear. All right, Bobby thought,
if Nam can be democratic, I can too. He looked down at
the title to see what Mr. Nam wanted them to learn.
"American English Hollywood Style," said the print on
the cover of the book.

"Mr. Nam . . . ," Bobby said.

"I know, I know," said Nam. "But give it a chance."

When he spoke he looked at the Goma again and Bobby
knew he was trapped. He opened the book at random,
and as he turned the pages he discovered that the book
was essentially a collection of old American slang phrases,
each one followed by a Korean explanation and by stick-
figure drawings depicting the social situations in which
the phrases could be used.

"Okeydokey," said Nam. "Here's one, page twenty-
six. What do such phrases mean?"

Everyone turned to page twenty-six, and Nam, before
sitting down again, patiently found the correct page for
the Goma. There were three English phrases on page

twenty-six, in the middle of a sea of tightly typed Korean. All the expressions were wrong and Bobby looked up, hoping someone would come to his aid. No such luck. "Explain please," said Mr. Nam, "each expression in turn."

Mr. Kwak had a faintly bemused smile on his face, but the others looked at Bobby as Nam did. "Nothing unreasonable going on here," their expressions seemed to say.

Bobby read the first phrase out loud, and to his surprise they all repeated it in unison: "Please may I have intercourse with you?"

He had them repeat the phrase one at a time, skipping the Goma, and reasonable renditions of "Please may I have intercourse with you?" rang around the table like a song. These folks had had language classes before.

"All right," he said, "what does this expression mean?" There was a moment of hesitation, but then, to his surprise, Miss Lee raised her hand.

"Yes?" Bobby said. "Miss Lee?"

"It is a polite method of asking for conversation," she said in good English.

Bobby's eyes lit up. "Yes!" he said. "That's right!"

"What, then, is the difference between 'intercourse' and 'speak?' " asked Mr. Soh.

"Ah," Bobby responded, "there's a big difference. Once they were similar but now they are not. Now we say speak every time."

"Except when being formal," said Mr. Nam.

"No, Mr. Nam. 'Please may I speak with you' is now accepted in informal and formal situations as well, you can be sure."

"What about when addressing the president of the United States?" Mr. Kwak wanted to know. His enigmatic smile was still there, but Bobby couldn't read his intentions.

"When addressing the president of the United States

one should never say, 'Please may I have intercourse with you,' " Bobby answered. Then he added, "Of this I am sure."

All five of them were taking notes, and even Mr. Nam seemed willing to alter the wording of his phrase now that Bobby had told him he should. Bobby could see, out of the corner of his eye, that the Goma was working his mouth a little too, turning it in completely unaccustomed ways.

Miss Lee got up to bring everyone tea and they went on to expression number two: "I always was born with a silver spoon in my mouth." Bobby read the phrase to them and they repeated it heartily. Maybe this isn't going to be so bad, he thought.

"This one comes a little closer to real usage," he said. "Except for that word 'always' in there. It means that the speaker was born rich, that he has always had money."

"Ah ha," said Mr. Nam. "You said 'always.' "

"Yes," Bobby answered, "but to say 'always was born' gives the impression of repeated action and we are only born once. It is an occurrence that ends once it has happened."

"Ah," said Mr. Nam, "but we can be reborn," and Mr. Kwak nodded, conceding, for Bobby, that point.

What was Bobby to do? If Nam was trying to draw him into religion, he would not be drawn. He looked at Mr. Lee, the only one as yet not to speak, but Mr. Lee shook his head. "Too deep," his expression seemed to say, his face froglike in the warming room.

Bobby took another breath and said slowly, "Perhaps we can be reborn and perhaps we cannot, but the expression in question has nothing to do with that. It has to do with whether or not the speaker was born rich, and one can only be born rich once. Thus, no 'always.' "

The English he had used was pretty complicated, but

no one seemed lost. Mr. and Miss Lee both nodded as if accepting the logic of the point, and Bobby stared at Mr. Nam, a bluff, hoping he'd shut up once he saw the challenge in his eyes. No such luck.

"Ah," Nam said quietly, "but when one is reborn one is reborn with abundance, and abundance means 'rich' so 'I always was born with a silver spoon in my mouth' means to be reborn, resplendent in the riches of God."

Bobby looked down at the Korean surrounding the expression in the book. Surely nothing like what Nam had said was represented there. What should he do? He had wanted this class to be his first real teaching success. The final expression leapt off the page as if mocking him, but he plunged ahead heedlessly out of his depth.

"Beat me daddy eight to the bar," he said, but this time there was only scattered repetition, for Mr. Nam and Mr. Soh were silent at the other end of the table.

"What the hell does this mean?" Bobby asked, and Mr. Kwak laughed. "It was apparently used when asking someone to dance," he said. And then he added, "I only know this, however, because I read a little ahead."

"Jesus Christ," said Bobby, but though he'd spoken under his breath, that was too much for Mr. Nam.

"Jesus Christ?" Nam said. "What do you mean by that?"

"Nothing, Mr. Nam," said Bobby. "I don't mean a goddamn thing by it." Nam leapt to his feet pointing down. "Jesus Christ! Goddamn!"

"Oh, shit," Bobby said.

Mr. Nam pulled at his collar with the hand that wasn't pointing and began to gag. He jumped up and down, his finger slicing the air like a concert master's.

Bobby tried to apologize for the language he had used but Mr. Nam would not quit. He stood there sputtering Bobby's obscenities back at him and then, plugging his ears against Bobby's attempts at reconciliation, he ran around collecting the copies of his book and bolted from the room. A moment later Mr. Soh ran out after him.

The rest of them sat there staring at each other. Bobby had wanted the evening to go so well. The expression on his face was one of desolation, and in a moment the three remaining teachers began touching him, bringing their chairs closer and telling him not to worry.

"Never mind," said Mr. Lee. "Nam is always like that," and Miss Lee nodded too, assuring Bobby that indeed he was. Then Mr. Kwak spoke.

"Now that that is over, what the three of us would really like is simply to discuss things with you." His tone was soft but there was an urgency in his voice that made Bobby think that everything, thus far, had gone according to his plan. "You know, we are Koreans," Mr. Kwak continued, "and there is much that we would like to say but cannot because we are afraid. Mr. Lee and Miss Lee, for example, would like to tell you about themselves. They both understand the English we have used and can make themselves understood when necessary." Mr. Kwak paused to see if Bobby was listening, if he had gotten over the shock of Mr. Nam's leaving, and then he added, "Do not misunderstand. We need not speak in English. As a matter of fact, we are all proud of your magnificent ability in Korean. But if we call it an English class, don't you see, that will make things easier all around. As for the real language of our discussions, it should be the truth, whatever the tongue."

Mr. Kwak stopped speaking and waited, but Bobby was stunned. Mr. Lee and Miss Lee both seemed to have transformed themselves from hopeful English students, from wide-eyed physical-education teachers, into conspirators, and Bobby didn't know what in the world to say. Peace Corps volunteers weren't supposed to be political, but then these people weren't asking him to be political, were they? They were only saying that they wanted to dispense with form and to talk openly.

Miss Lee had brought cake with her and she placed a fat piece in front of each of them, giving the Coma one from the portion she had brought for Mr. Soh and Mr. Nam. She looked at Bobby and said in a quiet, offhanded way, "You know, Mr. Lee and I are lovers."

It was only the second time Bobby had heard Miss Lee speak in English and he was sure she was mistaken in her choice of words. Perhaps "lovers," like "intercourse," had gone around the bend and come back with its meaning trimmed. Lovers meant friends perhaps, or maybe it meant that they were engaged.

He sat up and said, "What do you mean, exactly, when you use the word 'lovers.' Maybe you mean close friends?"

Miss Lee was still for a moment, but then she gave him a quizzical look. "Forgive me," she said. "Lovers. Mr. Lee and I are lovers." She emphasized her words carefully, and then Mr. Lee, hoping to make everything clear, closed his right fist and ran his left index finger in and out of it quickly, in an incredibly obscene way.

Bobby could feel himself growing red. "OK," he said. "I get it. Wow."

"We were lovers when we lived in Seoul," Miss Lee continued, "and we are lovers now. We will be lovers always, I think."

"So why don't you get married?" Bobby asked.

"Because our families are against us," Miss Lee said slowly. "Because Mr. Lee and I were sent to Taechon as punishment. We were banished for our activities when we were teaching elsewhere."

"You were banished together?" Bobby asked. "That was awfully nice of them."

"No, no," said Mr. Lee. "Banish apart. Come together two years later, secret-like."

"Mr. Lee changed his name," said Mr. Kwak. "After two years in another village he changed his name and was able to secure his position in Taechon. "I was the intermediary. Miss Lee had been here waiting for him all along."

Bobby looked at Mr. Lee. "What was your name before you changed it?" he asked.

"Mr. Lee," said Mr. Lee, and Bobby's double take made everyone laugh.

"Mr. Lee changed his given name, not his surname," said Miss Lee. "No need to change Mr. Lee. It is so common."

Though only minutes before Bobby had felt terrible about the disruption of his class, now he was feeling fine. Mr. Kwak seemed to sense the return of his good mood, for when he spoke again he said, "Please, Bobby, do not get the wrong idea. None of us are criminals here. Mr. and Miss Lee were student leaders, and I am only a country man struggling along with my languages and my verse. We are not North Korean sympathizers at all. Like most Koreans we are in favor of reunification someday, but all we want now is a clear voice. My thoughts concern the tragedy of our land, and Mr. and Miss Lee demonstrated to demand open elections, nothing more. One man, one vote. Do you recognize that slogan?" He sat up a little and grew intent. "Even now," he said, "even this conversation we could not have in Korean in any of the houses of this town. Any hint of curiosity about our brothers to the North, any comment concerning real elections with real candidates, would be dealt with harshly, to say the least."

Mr. Kwak had raised his voice and he sat back down now, a little chagrined at being carried away. "As you can see," he said, "this is something about which we care rather deeply."

Bobby certainly believed that, but when he looked at the Lees, with their bright eyes and their good health, the consummate physical-education teachers, he had a hard time reconciling himself to the fact that they were dissidents and lovers. Only Mr. Lee's gesture seemed in favor of it.

"So what is this English class for?" Bobby asked. "What do you want me to do?"

"What *can* you do?" asked Mr. Kwak. "What do you think?"

"Nothing," Bobby said. "The Peace Corps is just what it seems to be, nothing much, nothing special."

"Are you sure of that?" asked Miss Lee. "Some of us have wondered."

Bobby leaned back and smiled, looking at the Goma to share the wonder of it with him. What could they possibly think the Peace Corps was? If they had any idea that it was the C.I.A., as some Koreans believed, then they'd never have told him anything like they had. Surely they didn't believe it was some kind of leftist organization. What else was there?

"No, no," said Mr. Kwak, reading Bobby's smile. "We only want to get it off our backs. We know that you are what you appear to be. We only want a friend, an outlet. Otherwise everything stays bottled up."

"Get it off your chests," Bobby said, "not your backs." It was the first English mistake he'd heard Mr. Kwak make.

"Ah, yes," said Mr. Kwak, "quite."

Bobby didn't know what to do. They had been told in Seoul that they were to stay out of politics, that such involvement, in fact, was a sure ticket home. But was this politics? A couple of lovers who wanted free elections and an aging intellectual who wanted an outlet for his thoughts? No, this was not politics but ordinary human contact of the kind Bobby had rarely experienced at home.

"OK," he said, "so what should we talk about?" For some reason the three of them laughed.

"About poetry," said Mr. Kwak.

"About football," said Mr. Lee, "and judo."

"About Mr. Nam's funny book," said Miss Lee, "and about the Christian movement in general."

Bobby looked back at Mr. Lee. "I'd like to study judo," he said. "I've been thinking of talking to Policeman Kim."

"Talk to me," said Mr. Lee. "I can teach."

As suddenly as that the spirit of the little meeting had grown warm and humorous again, all three of them clearly glad to have said what they had, to have finally gotten what they had to say out in the open, off their backs or chests or whatever.

Bobby was about to suggest that they tell him about their hometowns when Mr. Kwak looked at his watch and said that it was time to go.

"What? Already?" Bobby asked.

"Yes," said Mr. Kwak, "time flies."

When they began looking around for their coats the Goma grew a little frantic. He closed his dirty fist around Miss Lee's sleeve and looked at her downright lewdly. "Beat me Daddy eight to the bar," he said. Mr. Nam had forgotten to take the book from the Goma, and Bobby was amazed at the sound. The Goma's intonation was accurate, his pronunciation clear, and in his eyes could be seen the tiniest flicker of real intelligence, before he dropped Miss Lee's arm and danced in little circles, moving around the room like a clown, picking up the last piece of cake and shoving it into his pocket like a fool.

Revolution

$$\overline{}\ \ \overline{}$$

Six in the second place means: When one's own day comes, one may create revolution.

A fter that bizarre evening at the library, Bobby went to school with new resolve, happy to have been embraced by his new friends and determined not to let the cold shoulder he was getting from Mr. Nam bother him. He taught well, and as time went by he met with his English club, studied Korean, and tried to stay away from the bars. He received disconcerting letters from his grandmother, saying Mrs. Nesbitt had been hospitalized because of her missing son and that the Royal Neighbors lodge was writing the White House on Mrs. Nesbitt's behalf, and in Bobby's answers to those letters he tried to let his newfound calmness show. But though he sent his sympathies to Mrs. Nesbitt, he could not find it within him to worry about Carl.

Three days a week Bobby went to a gym behind the police station and actually did begin studying judo with Mr. Lee. Bobby's fat, though diminishing, still pretty much hid the contours of his muscle, but Mr. Lee commented from the beginning on how strong he was. And he wasn't slow. For the first two weeks they did nothing but practice falls, and for a month after that they concentrated on the ankle sweep and the hip roll. It was fun and Judo Lee turned out to be a wonderful teacher. He was demanding and stingy with praise, but he was unfailingly kind as well. Judo Lee's friendship was a prize Bobby had not expected to win, and that he was learning to fight as well seemed like icing on the cake.

April, however, was the cruelest month again that year. Bobby had just come home from school one day when he happened to turn his radio on a little before his usual time. And the pandemonium of what he heard pierced him all the way from Memphis, Tennessee. Martin Luther King was dead, murdered by this guy James Ray.

Bobby had never considered Martin Luther King, but now that he was dead, Bobby looked around his room. He could picture the man's face and he knew the cadences of his voice well enough, but what else? The radio announcer wept, and as Bobby listened through the static and the tears he began to see America in ways he never had when living with his grandmother and thinking only of himself. Was it the era that made his country seem so torn or had it been that way always? He was shocked to understand that he really had no idea.

On the radio the magnitude of the tragedy seemed indisputable and Bobby tried to bring that level of anguish into his own room and mind. By the end of an hour he was sick at heart and sorry for Martin Luther King, but he fell asleep early anyway, finally knowing he'd be helpless to do anything, even if he were at home.

Still, Bobby had troublesome dreams that night, until just before midnight, when Cherry Consiliak came pounding on his door. The grandmother had awakened and gone out to open the gate, when Cherry's voice came into his room, making him sit up straight. Her Korean was poor and he recognized her voice immediately.

"Here I am!" Bobby shouted. "Cherry! Don't go!"

He was out of bed in an instant, pulling on his pants and stumbling into the wall. He had spoken too loudly, and the grandmother shushed him, pointing toward Policeman Kim's door. She then disappeared back into her own room, sliding under the covers next to her granddaughter once again.

"Cherry," said Bobby. "What's wrong? What's happened?" Despite her evident anguish, though, he couldn't help thinking she looked wonderful standing there.

"You didn't hear?" Cherry asked. "You don't know?"

Cherry's town was miles from Bobby's, far closer to Larry Corsio's. Had something happened to Larry then? he wondered.

"What?" he asked. "What is it?"

"It was on the radio. Martin Luther King is dead. Some white fucker shot him!"

"Oh," said Bobby. "Yeah, I heard."

"You heard? My God, Bobby, what are we going to do?"

Right then Bobby knew how little he understood, how clinically he'd reacted before. Cherry was brimming with grief, wrapped in it so completely that she was unaware she was wearing only a shawl against the cold. Bobby pictured her grabbing it as she ran out the door.

"Come in," he said, "it's late and we should be quiet."

Cherry let Bobby guide her into his room. She was crying quietly now, yet without restraint, and Bobby wanted more than anything to share it with her, to feel the loss too. How had he managed to lose touch with his emotions so, when she had hers there at her fingertips? He realized, as he watched her, that he had never been connected like this. He was nothing, a robot, as much affected by any old death as by this one.

"Now, now," he said, completely at a loss. "It's terrible, I know."

Cherry removed her shawl and looked around for something with which to wash her face. "Nice room," she said. "Do you have any water?" and Bobby was out the door instantly, out with his bucket to the well.

When he got back Cherry had composed herself a little. He wrung a washcloth out and carefully ran it across her face.

"It just seemed like it would work this time," she said, and Bobby nodded as if he knew what she meant. After that neither of them spoke for a while, though they sat under Bobby's covers and held each other a little to keep warm. But finally Cherry sighed and asked, "Why are there so many small-minded white shits in the world?" She looked up at Bobby as if she expected an answer.

"I don't know," he said. "Maybe the guy was crazy."

"He wasn't crazy, he was evil!" she hissed. "How the hell would you know? How the hell would you understand?"

By then it was one o'clock and Bobby was supposed to console Cherry Consiliak, the only black girl he had ever known and the woman he'd been thinking about for months, over the death of Martin Luther King, who was a legitimate hero, a true national leader whose fall really was tragic. And he had to teach school in six hours.

They were quiet for another long stretch, Cherry with her eyes closed, Bobby understanding that she needed him to hold her, when she spoke again, her voice a whisper.

"You've lost some more weight," she said, putting her arms around him. "I mean, really."

He had lost fifty pounds and he told her so. Policeman Kim had a scale. Because his skin was loose he still looked overweight, but the fact of the matter was that for the first time in his life he truly was not. He weighed only

two hundred and five pounds, seventy-five pounds
lighter than on the day of his military physical.

Cherry told him that she had lost weight too, placing
his hand along her rib cage to prove it. And when she
looked up to see his reaction he kissed her, clumsily laying
his broad face down on hers. It was the most unpremed-
itated thing he had ever done, and it was his first kiss.
He hoped desperately that she wouldn't misunderstand.

There was a moment when Cherry did misunderstand.
Bobby could feel it in her lips, which remained uncom-
mitted, as if waiting to taste the pureness of his motives.
"Could you possibly be using the death of Martin Luther
King to get laid, you white scumbag?" her lips seemed
to ask. But then they answered their own question by
finally kissing him back. And when it was over Cherry
sighed and then stunned him again by saying, "Hey,
Bobby, you're a virgin, right?"

Bobby was embarrassed as much by the matter-of-fact
tone of Cherry's question as by the words, and he said,
"What of it?" really hurt and surprised.

But Cherry was smart and caught herself immediately.
"Nothing, man," she said. "I was just asking. I'm sorry."
Then she snuggled up to him again, pulling his left hand
down onto her breast.

Cherry turned off the light and then undressed as cas-
ually as though she were alone. Bobby, trying to act as
nonchalant, nevertheless threw his clothes around wildly,
as if they had hot coals in them. This was the moment
he had dreamed of, though he had believed that it would
never come.

When they got back under the covers Bobby was shivering a little, and Cherry was careful, from the beginning,
not to appear to be his teacher. She muttered "Slowly" a
few times but was careful, even then, to appear to be
speaking to herself, and not to the frantic beating of his
exploding heart.

When they actually made love, every fiber of Bobby's body, every thought and feeling, every loose piece of tissue, was involved with it, finally no part of him holding back. Cherry kept her dark eyes open and she smiled with them whenever he looked, letting him know that for the moment, at least, he was alone with her in the world. Cherry made low, whimpering noises, but though Bobby's spirit rose and dashed about the world, all the while he didn't make a sound, only telling her once that he loved her when everything was finally done.

Bobby rose early the next morning, found the boy who was bad in English, and told him to tell the teachers at school that he was sick. It would be the first day of school he had ever missed.

It had always amazed Bobby that though there were six other people living in this house, he never ran into any of them. Now, though, with Cherry asleep under his quilt, they all appeared in the hallway together, falling over each other as if the house had suddenly grown small. Policeman Kim's wife had heard him telling her son that he'd be staying home and she lingered back, giving instructions all around. The grandmother, who had seen Cherry come in, knew that he wasn't sick and said something fast, which made them all fall silent once again. And Heh Sook, the little girl, positioned herself so that she'd have a chance of seeing Cherry, should Bobby open his door again.

Cherry, when she finally awoke, looked great. She found a T-shirt to pull on over her nakedness, but it did nothing to cool Bobby's ardor. "You don't have to wake up yet," he said. "It's early and I've just told them I'm not going to school."

Cherry yawned. "Do you have a substitute teacher?" she asked. "Is there a substitute teacher at your school?"

Bobby thought about it, but he didn't know. In fact, he

could not remember any teacher having been absent before. What did they do when someone was ill? "Do you?" he asked. "Is there a substitute teacher where you work?"

"No," said Cherry. "The other teachers cover. It cuts way down on absenteeism."

Daylight was at the window, and Bobby closed the curtains tightly before he sat back down, hoping Cherry would want to make love again. She seemed relaxed now, but when she did let him under the covers she put her arms around him again quickly before telling him another bit of news.

"I'm thinking about quitting, Bobby," she said. "I'm thinking about going home."

"No," said Bobby.

Cherry laughed. "Hey," she said, "we never see each other anyway."

Bobby tried to think fast. It was Martin Luther King's death that had depressed her enough to make her want to leave. Life in Korea was hard enough when things were fine. He had to think of something quick, to make her change her mind.

"I'll go with you," he said.

Cherry laughed again, for the first time regaining a little of her old spirit. "You? What would you do at home—march for civil rights?"

Bobby could think of nothing to say to that, so he asked, "How many of us have left by now?"

"Sixteen," said Cherry. "So leaving's no big deal. Besides, my town doesn't need an English teacher. I'd be doing them a favor."

"No, you wouldn't," he said. "And none of these towns need English teachers, so what the hell."

"You really want to quit with me, Bobby? Come off and be my babe?" She was teasing, but at least she was cheerful. Now his job was twofold: to keep her happy and to make her stay.

"I don't want you to go," Bobby said. "We could see each other every week. We could see Larry more often too."

Cherry smiled. "Larry quit," she said.

"What? He did not!"

"Sure did, just last week. He was the sixteenth."

Bobby was speechless. Why hadn't he heard?

"Anyway," said Cherry, "that's not the point. Even if nobody quit I still would. That fucking man has shot Martin Luther King, and the Peace Corps is no place for me now. Things aren't fine at home; my own house is not in order."

Bobby stopped when she spoke, though he'd formed a line of arguments a mile long in his head. Maybe she should quit. And if she shouldn't, then why shouldn't she?

"Really, Cherry, I don't know," he said, but she could hear the change in his voice and she immediately pulled him to her, kissing his cheek.

"I knew you'd understand," she said. "I knew it!"

After that the day passed quickly. They made love again, this time Cherry clearly the teacher, and then Bobby went into the kitchen to ask the maid to fix them eggs and toast. Cherry talked about growing up in Philadelphia. She had been young for her class, she said. She had been studious and conservative and had gone away to college though most of her friends had not. She'd wanted to be a writer, a journalist, and had thought that the Peace Corps would broaden her, giving her a sense of the world. And as she talked Bobby thought, God, what a wonderful woman. Would she finish the term, he asked, would she stay until June at least? But she said she couldn't say. Martin Luther King had been an idol of hers, did he understand that? This was no ordinary loss. Martin Luther King had been larger than life, so his death was larger too. She had heard him speak in Washington and had thought of going South a time or two, to Selma and Montgomery.

To Bobby, Cherry was the most beautiful woman on earth. Again they made love, the house, meanwhile, as quiet as a tomb. Cherry waited, at his pleading, until the last train that night, though it took triple the time to get home. Even when leaving the station, the train did so at a snail's pace, so Bobby was able to walk along beside it, holding Cherry's hand until the platform ended.

When he came out of the station, the Goma and the biting woman were standing there chatting and they gave Bobby kindly looks. "Good evening, look at the sky, maybe the weather's finally going to break," their looks seemed to say. The biting woman didn't ask for money and the Goma wasn't carrying his English book. Normally Bobby would have walked quickly away, but that evening he stood there with them for a while. It really was warmer. He tried to hold Cherry's face in his mind, the sound of her train leaving in the channels of his ears. He turned a little in the street, almost a dance, and for a while his heart felt as large as his body once had been.

Grace

== ==
== ==

*Six in the fifth place means: Keeping his jaws
still. The words have order.*

Some weeks after Cherry's visit Mr. Kwak and
the Lees came to Bobby's room for another
meeting. Mr. Kwak had an anxious-looking face, and
when they were all settled he began immediately to speak,
waiting only for the departure of Policeman Kim's maid,
who had come into the room with tea.

"Next week there is a special day at school," he said,
looking directly at Bobby. "It is called spy-catching day
and it is a travesty. It builds roadblocks to clear thought
in the minds of our students."

Taken by surprise Bobby repeated, "Spy-catching day?"
and when he did so Miss Lee jumped in. "You have given
us great courage," she said. "Because of you we are going
to boycott spy-catching day."

Bobby had no idea what to say. What had he done to
give them courage?

"What's spy-catching day?" he asked, and to his surprise it was Mr. Lee who attempted a clarification.

"Very strange day indeed," he said. "Headmaster Kim

find out-of-towner to come around wearing long coat and funny shoes. Out-of-towner try buying cigarette or try entering public bath without knowledge of pricing system in Republic of Korea. Middle-school student search for him everywhere. And whosoever discover him win big prize, becoming anticommunist hero."

Bobby looked from Mr. Lee to the others, but they were all solemn. Was this what they'd been planning to tell him all along, the real reason they'd wanted to form the group?

"And you are going to boycott the day," he said. "Won't that get you in trouble?"

"More than trouble," said Miss Lee. "It will cost us our jobs."

The maid came back, breaking the tension by pouring more tea and passing around a little tray of rice balls, but Mr. Kwak motioned her out of the room again.

"You may not see any importance in this," he said. "Such a silly day, such a silly, backward country. But we are teachers and feel we must stand up for the rights of the students in our school. Free speech really begins with free thought. Spy-catching day is a small example of the way our government hinders free thought, but it is a good one. And we feel that if we oppose it, maybe others will follow. All we have to give our students is the example that we set. Don't you see?"

Bobby did see, but he had no idea what to say. He was touched that they confided in him, but Mr. Kwak was right, it really did seem silly. Finally he managed to ask, "Which day is it? Which day next week?"

"Wednesday," said Miss Lee. "Spy-catching day is always the same. It breaks up the week for the teachers."

The insight Bobby had into the nature of his three friends was temporarily lost, however, two days before spy-catching day when he heard reports from America of Robert Kennedy's assassination. Teachers he'd never spoken to shook their heads and laid hands on his shoulders. "Such a violent country," they said. "And such a young man. The brother of the president."

It was Monday evening when the news reached Korea, and the next morning Headmaster Kim called Bobby into his office. "Not a good year for your country," he said. "First the Tet Offensive, then the death of that good black man, and now this."

"Yes," said Bobby. "It's a terrible year for my country."

He did feel terrible about the death of Robert Kennedy. The Voice of America had broadcast Kennedy's victory speech from that Los Angeles hotel, and Bobby had turned his radio on in the middle of it. He had heard the assassin's handgun popping its static over the airwaves, and he had cried, alone in his room, when the announcer told him that Robert Kennedy was dead. Kennedy was the man who would have ended the war, saving guys like Ron and Gary and, who knows, perhaps bringing back Carl Nesbitt too. Bobby understood it all.

Headmaster Kim saw the grief in his eyes and was offering to let him take the next day off to mourn. Bobby thought about it for a moment. Since the next day was spy-catching day there were no classes to teach, and he would have taken the day off, had it not been for the Lees and Mr. Kwak. Tomorrow was their big day. They had told him about the boycott, so were he not to show up they would think he had stayed away because of it.

"That's very kind," he said, "but I feel my duty is to remain at school."

That day Bobby's students were full of questions about how Americans could kill their leaders so easily, and when he walked into his best class the monitor bowed deeply and presented him with a letter. "I AM SORRY," the letter said, and below these three English words were the signatures of all the students in the room.

"Thank you," Bobby told them. "I am sorry too."

This was English they could understand and the students smiled down at their desks. "I am sorry. I am sorry too," some of them whispered.

As Bobby stood in front of his class, though, he began to think of Cherry. When Martin Luther King was killed she'd decided to quit the Peace Corps, saying that his death was personal enough to make her want to go home and get involved in civil rights. Should he feel that way now, then, about Robert Kennedy? Was it his being white that made Kennedy's death pierce him so; was it King's blackness that primarily moved Cherry? Would Kennedy's death mean to Cherry precisely what Martin Luther King's had meant to him? Bobby had not seen Cherry since that night in his room, but couldn't he run to her now, letting her comfort him in turn?

Bobby looked up at his students and said, "You know, in order to become president of the United States you have to pass a test in Korean." He had no idea where such a statement came from, but there it was, the strangest possible lie in the face of what Headmaster Kim had called his personal tragedy and what North Korean radio had labeled, "America's continued running-dog murder of its few good men."

"What?" said the student. "Ha! Don't pull our legs."

"Not really," he said, but the students hadn't heard.

"In Korean?" asked their monitor. "They must pass a test in Korean?"

The students were incredulous and talked among themselves. Bobby often joked with them, they knew that. When the repetition of English got boring he would often switch to Korean in order to tell them some wild story, completely made-up. But he was sad now and they knew that too. Could he possibly be joking at a time like this?

The best student raised his hand, everyone's questions forming in him.

"Uh, who got the highest score?" he asked.

"Sorry?"

"In Korean. Which one got the highest grade?"

"Robert Kennedy," Bobby said, trying to bring his lie around to stand for something good.

A murmur went up and the spokesman came back to him. "What about Nixon?" he asked. "We all know him. What score did Nixon get?"

"Nixon barely passed," Bobby responded quietly. "He got the lowest score."

Another boy asked, "Who was second? After Robert Kennedy, who was next?"

"McCarthy was second," said Bobby. "You may not know him but he's becoming popular now."

This was absolutely crazy. News of the Korean test he'd made up would be all over school the moment class was out. He was supposed to be grieving over the death of Robert Kennedy, not making up terrible lies. Had he learned nothing over the passing weeks, nothing from Cherry? Though skin hung loosely from his body now, he felt the fat come back. What was there, within him, that brought out such awful impulses as these?

Bobby looked up at the waiting students. "Eugene McCarthy," he said. "He's the one."

"Yes! Yes!" the students called. "We hope he wins! McCarthy with the highest score in Korean! Good for McCarthy! He's a good man!"

They were on their feet when the bell rang, shouting McCarthy's name and striding into the halls with it on their tongues. This was the day's last class and when Bobby got back to the teachers' room he could still hear the students shouting as they marched across the outside field.

Bobby sat at his desk feeling bad when Mr. Nam put a hand on his shoulder, speaking to him for the first time in months.

"I am very sorry."

Bobby looked up. "Don't mention it," he said, "thank you."

"You can't teach an old dog new tricks," said Nam. "Who is this man McCarthy?"

"One of the presidential candidates," Bobby said. "A Democrat." He picked up his books and stood, hoping to get out before Mr. Nam, of all people, took him to task. None of the teachers had left yet but surely he could, on a day like today. Headmaster Kim would understand.

But Mr. Nam, still chin-fisted and worried, followed Bobby when he went into the hall. While Bobby was putting on his shoes Mr. Nam spoke again.

"What was McCarthy's score?" he asked.

"Eighty percent," Bobby told him.

"And Nixon?"

"Low. Under fifty percent."

Bobby had his shoes on but Mr. Nam had slipped into his shoes too, clearly planning to walk Bobby to the gate.

It was such a beautiful day and Bobby felt so rotten. If not for Mr. Kwak and the Lees he could have taken the next day off, riding the train to Cherry's village where he could regain himself, stop the backsliding and grow. He needed someone to talk to but it had to be an American.

He was almost off the school grounds when Mr. Nam spoke again. "Tell me," he said. "In which other languages are they tested, these candidates?"

"Only a few," Bobby answered.

"French? Spanish?" asked Mr. Nam.

"Yes," Bobby said, passing through the gate.

"What about Arabic?" asked Nam. He was leaning through the gate, cupping his hand and calling.

"No," Bobby said. "Not Arabic."

"What about Japanese? Surely if Korean, then Japanese!"

"Yes," Bobby said, "that too."

He wanted to run but he merely kept his head low, and didn't turn back.

"What about Hebrew?" shouted Nam. "What about Russian?"

Bobby didn't answer but Nam kept calling and in a moment his persistence brought a few children out.

"What about Finnish?" said Mr. Nam's distant voice. "And what about Chinese?"

His voice stirred the children and they began to skip, keeping up with Bobby's fast pace.

"What about hello, OK?" one of them asked, and Bobby turned on the child, frightening him. "What about Serbo-Croatian?" Mr. Nam called, one last time, "What about lies?"

Bobby was halfway home by the time Mr. Nam finally stopped. When he turned to look he could see Nam's head still sticking out of the school gate, but it was a quiet head, not even trying to shout.

What was all this? Was it his job to lie to everyone, making light of serious matters, just as the fat that had always surrounded him had begun to give way like it had, to the thin man whom he'd never suspected was inside? He resolved to take spy-catching day off and to go see Cherry after all. He would send word back to Headmaster Kim with the boy who was bad in English. And when he returned on Thursday he would see Mr. Kwak and the Lees and try to explain. He was an American, after all, and in times of trouble he really did have to get together with someone who would understand and talk about the awful times at home.

When one lives one's life in pursuit of scholarship and understanding, it is the highest and most honorable of paths—any fool knows that. And though I did not meet my goal of becoming either a college professor or a government official, I have not done so badly. I am a teacher and an administrator in a provincial school. When I walk through the town people stop to greet me, many of them bowing, many more remembering that they were my students and silently thanking me for what I did.

Now, though, my sense of things is being undermined by this American. There was another assassination in his country and I do not fully understand his attitude. He was in the headmaster's office for a long while, and when the headmaster offered him a day off and his own profound sympathy, the American turned it down—the day off, I mean. Of course, anyone can understand that he did so out of loyalty to the school, but who can understand these ridiculous jokes of his? They are barbaric, they show a cruel heart, and Mr. Nam has started a campaign against him because of them, insisting on calling them lies.

What am I to do? I want to come to the American's defense, but I do not know how. When Mr. Nam asked me for my opinion on the thing I was able to put him off, but I know he will ask again. What am I to say? How can I defend such behavior in the face of a man's frivolous understanding of his place? Think of what it must mean. If a man does not understand his relationship to his rulers, which is primary, then how can he understand anything else?

I am still drawn to our American teacher. I still want, somehow, to be of help to him, but I am perplexed and unhappy with today's turn of events.

Written at the Pleasant Feeling Tearoom again, as I put off going home, hoping that the tearoom's name will influence the darkness of my mood.

4301 年　　4 月　　8 日

The Clinging Fire

Six in the fifth place means: Tears in floods, sighing and lamenting. Good fortune.

Bobby took the night train, hoping to get to Cherry's town early enough to find her house and knock on her door. But as he neared the town he grew tentative. Would she be glad to see him? Were these things reversible, the midnight visits of mourning friends? Was he in fact mourning, or did he just want to see her?

He worried all the way to Chonan, but when he got off the train and came out of the station it was not yet ten, and his mood expanded. He asked a young cab driver if he knew where the American black girl lived, and the driver said that though he did not, he had seen her often enough. He said he knew her tearoom so Bobby got in his cab.

"She's pretty, eh, the black girl?" said the driver.

"Are you sure you know the right tearoom?" Bobby asked.

The driver didn't answer, but in less than a minute he pulled up in front of the DeLuxe Tearoom. "Do you want me to wait?" he asked. "If you want me to I can wait a while."

Bobby said that waiting would be fine and went inside. This tearoom, despite its name, was shabbier than his own.

"Ah," said a woman. "You must be Miss Ko's friend."

Peace Corps volunteers were often given Korean names. Bobby nodded and asked, "Do you know where she lives?"

"I do," said the woman, "but she's out of town."

"It's the middle of the week," Bobby said. "Doesn't she have to work tomorrow?"

"Miss Ko's not working anymore," said the tearoom woman. "She and her headmistress argued and she quit."

"Where did she go?" he asked, alarmed.

"I don't know," said the woman, "but perhaps up to the American base. She and her friend only left this afternoon." Bobby thanked the woman and hurried back outside. If Cherry had a friend, then who could that friend be but Gary Smith? He imagined Ron's truck, Cherry popping in to say good-bye. The taxi was idling at the curb, and when he got in he asked the driver if he knew the American base, down the coast, near Hongsong.

"Sure," the driver said.

Bobby asked how much it would cost to go there, and the driver eyed him carefully for the first time. "If we had time I'd take you for two thousand won," he said. "But curfew is near. I won't be able to get back."

"OK," said Bobby. "Two thousand won plus a room for the night. You can drive back tomorrow."

The driver nodded, but said that he wanted to stop by his farm first and tell his wife. His farm was on the Hongsong road, not far out of the way.

For Bobby's part, though he wanted him to floor it, he had no choice but to agree to the stop. He couldn't get back down the coast by train, and he had to catch up with Cherry before she left the country altogether. He was anxious and obsessed but luckily the driver turned out to be fast. They were only on the road for fifteen minutes when they got to his farm's turnoff. Not seeing any lights, Bobby asked how far it was.

"Up there," said the driver, "bottom of that hill."

The new road was flat and in the distance Bobby could see the dark shape of a low mountain, where this driver's farm was presumably nestled.

Though he had ridden in the back of the cab when going from the station to the tearoom, when he came back out he'd climbed into the front. Now he looked at the driver suspiciously. Was he in danger, riding alone with this man? They were already miles from town, after all, and the driver was young and tough-looking. He had a tooth missing in the front of his mouth and was wearing only a T-shirt under his open coat.

"Have you been driving a taxi long?" Bobby asked. "Have you always lived around here?"

"I drive at night," the driver answered. "Mornings I practice Tae Kwon Do, teach a little, kick around."

As Bobby looked at the man's hands on the wheel, he made out the rough outline of their calluses. He was driving into the hills with a martial arts man, and he had all his money in his flimsy old wallet. Still, he banked on the man's cheerfulness: surely a mugger wouldn't be so talkative.

The hill was still some distance away, but just as Bobby was about to complain, the cab stopped a few meters off the road. "Be right back," said the driver, and Bobby's heart eased when he saw a dark house out the window to his left.

The driver jumped from the car and ran into the darkness calling someone's name. In a moment a lamp was lit and a mournfully weak light emanated from the house. Bobby sat in the cab trying to glean meaning from the sounds he heard, but five minutes passed, and then ten, and the house fell silent. What was happening? he wondered. Had this guy been married so short a time that he was in there making love while Bobby waited in the car? And come to think of it, it was unlike a Korean man ever to worry about telling his wife anything. Had Bobby thought of that on the road he would really have been frightened.

Opening the door, Bobby stepped halfway out of the car and called to the guy, who called right back, "Coming!" And since he was out of the car, he took a deep breath and looked around. It was really beautiful territory, a beautiful country, Korea. The hill behind the house loomed magnificently, its menace contributing to the wonder of the place. Mr. Kwak had always said that the sky was high, and for the first time Bobby felt he knew what he meant. The stars seemed farther away than they did in America. They were bright but were made smaller as if by increased distance. And they seemed dashed more haphazardly across the sky, like salt across the surface of a lacquered box.

Bobby stood looking at the sky and marveling at the amazing randomness of things. Who could have predicted, this morning, that he'd be at the home of a cab driver or riding through the unknown hills tonight?

"Hey! OK! Sorry to keep you waiting," said the driver, and Bobby was brought back from his stargazing when he realized that the driver was not alone. He had a woman with him and she, in turn, was carrying a small pink bag.

"You don't mind, I hope," said the driver. "But we haven't been to the base in months."

"Howdy," said the wife. "You go base? Base number one."

No wonder it had taken them so long. In the weak light from the cab of the car Bobby saw that this driver's wife was dressed to kill, in tight, tight, pants and a red sweater with huge pink hearts surrounding each breast. And the driver too had changed into a suit, black shirt, white tie.

"I can't believe, really," said the wife. "I used to live that base. To go back will be fine, what good luck."

She smiled and slid in the driver's side, so all three of them were in the front seat of the cab. Her hair was cut like Cleopatra's, straight across her forehead and straight across the back of her neck.

The driver wasted no time getting back to the main road again. His wife was carrying a floppy hat and she put it on now, holding it down with the hand nearest the driver while pinching Bobby's thigh with the other. "Slow down, honey," she said, but Bobby was just as happy with the speed. Maybe they really would get there before curfew, and maybe this Tae Kwon Do guy wouldn't see his wife's right hand on his leg.

As they flew down the road, the stars and the looming mountain receded and the June dust ballooned behind them and all around. The wife was chatty and the driver was fast. "Don't worry, honey, he don't speak English," she said.

By train the trip would have taken two hours, but by cab it was far faster. And though he had spoken on the way from town, the driver seemed content now to let his wife do the talking. "I miss it, you know, the life," she said. "Lots of beer and money, sleep late every day. I almost marry G.I. two time, one black, one white. I never in my life thought I end up with Korean."

She was lost for a while in how wonderful her old life had been, but then she laughed and, turning to her husband, actually translated for him what she'd been telling Bobby. He laughed too, glancing around with his cheerful eyes.

"Can you believe?" the wife continued. "I used to be Gloria, now Mrs. Kim. Life fucking strange sometime."

Lord, yes, thought Bobby, and then the driver rolled

his wife Bobby's way by sharply turning left. They were
past Hongsong in a flash and onto the missile-base road.
Ron's truck made the trip in about twenty minutes, but
Bobby had the feeling they'd be there in five. It was only
eleven o'clock. They had curfew beat by a mile.

Mrs. Kim, the Gloria of old, was too excited to talk once
they got near the Vil. And when they stopped she jumped
from the cab and held both arms up in the air. Bobby
expected her to yell, "Gloria's back!," but she stretched,
turning the gesture into a yawn when no one noticed her.
   The Vil was Bobby's true destination, for he was sure
that Cherry couldn't be on the base. That Thanksgiving
dinner had been a special occasion, and he knew that
even as Gary's guest she wouldn't find such easy access
again. But though Bobby could have found the hooches
during the day, at night he wasn't so sure. He had expected the Vil to be quiet on a weeknight but it was
raucous. They were in front of a bar called the Lucky
Seven Club, which was packed.
   Mr. Kim locked his taxi and joined them on the boardwalk and Bobby gave him two thousand won.
   "Wait," said Gloria. "Let's have a drink first. See the
town. The three of us."
   She was smiling so happily that Bobby thought it
wouldn't hurt to settle them inside the bar and then ask
around for the hooches. It was a small place, after all,
and he should be able to find Cherry in a second.
   Inside the Lucky Seven Club, all the tables were taken
and a three-man band was playing in the corner. The
customers were mostly American soldiers, but they were
celebratory, no sense of Robert Kennedy's death anywhere.
   "Order some beer," Bobby said. "I want to look
around." But before he could get away Gloria slipped her

arms around his waist, grabbed the loose skin that was there, and pressed into him down low.

"You good guy," she said. "Forgive my always touchy before. Old habit die slow."

Bobby quickly forgave her. She really was great-looking, especially in this light, and he could tell she'd been disappointed that no one had recognized her. "I'll be back," he said. "I just have to find someone."

"What's her name?" Gloria asked. "Maybe I know her, remember from before."

"Her name's Cherry. But she wasn't here before."

Gloria thought back, trying to remember whether there had been a Cherry or not and Bobby left, mumbling again that he would return and stepping out the door.

Immediately an old madam saw him. "Nice girl everywhere," she said. She looked at her watch, giving the first indication that anybody was thinking of the curfew. "Getting late," she said. "All night ten dollar."

"I'm looking for someone," said Bobby. "Do you know Gary Smith's hooch?"

"Gary Smith hooch? Sure."

"Where is it?" he asked.

She sighed and pointed up toward the base's gate. "International Club," she said. "Turn left, down alley."

Bobby started toward the International Club, but then looked once again at the madam. "Gloria's back," he said. "Did you see her? She's inside the Lucky Seven Club right now." The woman didn't speak, but her expression lightened, and as Bobby left she was walking back through the Lucky Seven Club's door.

It was only a block to the International Club, but girls came down off the boardwalk, some of them only whispering but others trying to grab Bobby and drag him home. It was late and hunting season was almost over.

When he got to the club and turned into the row of

hooches things got worse. Here there were lots of low doorways with girls in front of every one. These were awful places, really, and some of the girls were made up to look like walking versions of their rooms, with green makeup if the hooches were green and psychedelic swirls on their faces if the walls of their rooms were wild. Some of the girls called out, but Bobby didn't respond. At least he knew he was near Gary's place when he heard Mississippi John Hurt again, singing Cherry's old song.

> "Got to go to Memphis,
> From there to Leland.
> Got to see my baby,
> 'Bout a lovin' spoonful."

Bobby had become so involved with Mr. Kim and Gloria that he'd neglected to consider what he might find here. It was late, maybe he shouldn't have come. Gary had as much as told him he was interested in Cherry too. Feeling like an intruder, that he should go home, he hesitated in front of the hooch. He then knocked quickly, four rapid taps.

"Yeah?" called Gary. "Who's there?"

"It's me, Bobby. May I come in?"

Bobby couldn't hear anything over the music, but in a moment Gary opened the door. He stood in the half-light with a newspaper in his hand, and though Bobby could not see past him he was immediately sure he was alone. "Bobby," said Gary. "What the hell? What's going on?"

"I'm looking for Cherry. I got the day off because of this Robert Kennedy thing. . . . Have you heard the news?"

"I'm reading about it now," said Gary. "It's in the *Stars & Stripes* already." He paused. "Cherry's gone, Bobby," he said. "She left about an hour ago for home."

Bobby stepped into the hooch and Gary closed the door. "She came up here this afternoon and I got her on a troop truck heading straight for Kimpo," he said.

Bobby looked down and asked to see the paper. There was a photograph of the guy who'd shot Robert Kennedy on the front page, and Robert Kennedy was there too, his stricken face difficult to see in the bad light.

Bobby wanted only to leave now. Before he could speak, though, there was another knock on the door. God, wasn't it curfew yet, he thought. Gary called out, but when there was no answer he opened the door to find Gloria, Mr. Kim, and the madam Bobby'd met right behind her. The madam was carrying a tray with watermelon on it. Next to the watermelon was a plate of strawberries and a bowl of powdered sugar.

"Ah, Smith," she said, "looky here. Your friend bring Gloria back. We make a little treat, say thanks."

Gary looked at Bobby strangely, but moved back out of the way.

Gloria came in first. "I can't believe," she said. "It like a dream, really. One minute home in bed, next minute back like nothin' happen. Like no time go by." She turned in the room, expressing the freedom she felt, but then stopped. "Hello, Gary," she said softly. "How do you do?"

"Hello, Gloria," said Gary Smith.

Bobby sat against the cushions of the room, hollow-chested but smiling up at the others. The madam, it turned out, was Gary's landlady and Gloria had lived next door. When Gary'd first arrived in Korea, her beauty seduced him early, bringing him out to the Vil, and estranging him from his fellow officers who never left the base. Gloria had been Gary's neighbor and girlfriend whom Bobby had brought back because she was now the wife of the taxi driver he had chosen to carry him into all of this. And he had arrived too late. Cherry Consiliak was gone.

While they ate the watermelon Bobby chimed in from time to time, his mouth spewing words into the room. After the madam left, though, he asked Gary what was going on in Ron's hooch, and was told that Ron was on base, getting ready to be transferred to Seoul. He would have asked if Gloria and Mr. Kim could sleep there, but Gloria touched him once again. "Don't worry, honey," she said. "Mama got a room for us. Mr. Kim sleepy now, we go back soon. Maybe meet for a beer at Mama's once Mr. Kim asleep." As the two of them stood to leave Gloria added, "Don't forget, I wait for you both outside. . . ."

But when the door closed, Bobby was suddenly as tired as Mr. Kim. All this pretense was making him ill. Cherry was gone, Robert Kennedy was dead, and if he'd stayed in Taechon he'd have been asleep hours ago, ready to support his friends in the morning for their boycott of spy-catching day.

He was feeling devastated and tired but was cheered a little when Gary Smith got up and left the room too. "I'll go find her," he said. "If you feel like it, come on over to Mama's for a beer."

The light was out, the music was off, and Bobby had fallen asleep when the door opened again and Gloria came in. She quickly slipped into the bed beside him, her hands roaming all over his body before she understood that it wasn't Gary she was touching but Bobby, who was quickly waking up from a dream.

"Gloria!" he said. "What are you doing here? What about Mr. Kim?"

"Mr. Kim sleep like dead," she said. "I been six month on that farm. Where Gary?"

"He went out to look for you. What time is it? Are you sure Mr. Kim's asleep?"

"No problem," said Gloria. "Not really married anyhow. Just together for convenience sake."

"What if he comes looking for you?"

Gloria seemed to think about this for a moment, and Bobby decided that the best thing for him to do would be to get dressed again and go outside. He really didn't want Mr. Kim coming in, married or not.

"I'll go find Gary," he said. "You'd better come along." He didn't know what else to say. If he left her, he knew she'd be there when he got back.

Gloria was stroking Bobby's arm, considering whether to settle for him, but when Bobby stood and pulled on his pants, she sighed and stood up too. "Can you believe?" she said. "After all this time Gary Smith still here. Mr. Kim no problem at all."

The pathway in front of the hooch was pitch dark, and when Bobby started to speak Gloria put her hand over his mouth. "Curfew very bad news," she whispered.

They walked to the end of the row, where the madam's room apparently was, but when they stopped in front of it, the only sound they heard was coming from a bucket of cold water under a dripping tap. Suddenly, though, Gary materialized, coming out from somewhere and standing beside them like a ghost.

"Hi," he said.

Bobby jumped, but Gloria grabbed Gary's arm. "Oh Gary, where you been?" she asked. "Come on, let's go back inside."

"What about Mr. Kim?" asked Gary Smith.

There was no moon, though Bobby remembered that there had been when, so many hours before, he'd stood out from the taxi at Mr. Kim's farm. When Gloria turned Gary toward his hooch, Bobby stayed back, letting the darkness surround him. If he stood just in the center of the path he could not see the hooch doors, and if he looked up he could not see the sky, and there was mud below his feet from where the tap bucket had overflowed. He waited until he could no longer hear Gary and Gloria ahead, and then he followed them. Only he went past Gary's door and stepped into Ron's hooch, where the walls were painted black like the night outside.

When Bobby kicked off his shoes and pulled the filthy blankets around him, he was alone again in a world of his own. In the other world Robert Kennedy had died and Mrs. Nesbitt's son was missing. And an hour ago Cherry Consiliak had left for home. But it wasn't Bobby's intention to dwell on any of that. His intention, rather, was to wonder for the ten-thousandth time how people could pass through his life so easily, marking him with their presence but taking nothing of him with them when they left.

Waiting

≡≡ ≡≡

Six at the top means: One falls into the pit.
Uninvited guests arrive.

W hen Bobby stepped off the train the next evening, the Goma was waiting for him, and
his expression was not one of peace. "Where have you
been?" he asked. "Didn't you know today was special?"

"I had to see somebody," said Bobby. "Why? What
happened? Who was the spy? Who caught him?"

"The whole thing's been called off, put back until tomorrow. But the spy's in town somewhere, hiding out."

Bobby thought of Mr. Kwak and the Lees. "Why did
they postpone it?" he asked.

The Goma looked at him carefully. "Because tomorrow
is market day. Strangers will be coming to town and the
streets will be confused. It's cheating to use a farmer for
the spy, but we all think they will. And farmers always
act like fools. Who'd know whether they were supposed
to be spies or not?"

"So nothing happened at school? They just had an ordinary day?"

The Goma shrugged and turned, taking the bank note

Bobby'd given him over to the biting lady and then joining Bobby as he headed up the street. "There's a bet on that again this year it won't be a school kid who finds him. Not for two years has it been a school kid. It's always one of us finding him and then selling the information. School kids get money from their papas and pay us off."

Bobby eyed the Goma walking along. He was so upset by this postponement that even his Korean was clarified by it. Once they reached Miss Moon's tearoom Bobby turned to take him in for tea. He found the door locked, though, and the light off. He had never known the tearoom to be closed before, but he was too exhausted for tea anyway, and since it wasn't late he wanted to go home and get his towel and soap. The public bath was open until eleven and he knew he'd have the place to himself.

"Well, good luck tomorrow," he said. The Goma stepped closer and lowered his voice. "You know who it is, don't you?"

"No," said Bobby. "How would I know? I've been gone."

"Everyone knows that the headmaster chooses. We've got guys watching his house every minute but he's tricky. Come on, who is it? I know he told you."

"Be serious. No one tells me anything around here. I'd be the last one he would tell."

The Goma gave Bobby a measured look, before he nodded and slumped off in the direction of the inn. "I've got to sleep," he said. "This whole thing starts early. . . ."

When Bobby got home, it seemed like everyone he knew had been there. The grandmother had notes and spoke to him so fast that he couldn't catch all of what she said. He did gather, however, that Headmaster Kim had been by, and that there was a message from Seoul, news of some trouble, or even, the grandmother whispered, a death. Bobby was to call the headmaster immediately. His phone number was 007—perfect for spy-catching day, Bobby reflected—so he went into Policeman Kim's room and asked the operator to connect him. No one was home at the headmaster's, but when he came out, the grandmother looked at him with poised hands anyway, ready to tear her hair for whatever the bad news had been. A chance to mourn was an important release, and when Bobby said he'd try again after his bath she was upset. "What?" she said. "You'd better wait right here. Go to the bath tomorrow."

She actually tried to stop him from finding clean clothes and a towel, and he had to dodge her at the door. As a partial apology, he called over his shoulder that he would hurry.

When Bobby got to the public bath he paid his thirty won and went inside. Taechon had three baths but this was the only one he'd ever used. The Goma, in fact, had first brought him here, though the Goma had never been inside himself.

The first room was lined with wooden lockers and benches, reminding Bobby of the ancient high school he'd attended at home. Somehow the grandmother's foreboding hadn't affected him much. Surely no one was dead. His real grandmother was too healthy to be in danger, and who was left?

Bobby had put his clothes in the locker and walked into the steaming bath room itself before, suddenly, the thought struck him that the call he had received concerned Cherry Consiliak. Cherry was dead on the road, or killed in some accident while waiting at Kimpo for her airplane ride home. Why else would he get a call from Seoul?

Bobby cried out once in the empty room, but finally he controlled himself and sat on a stool at the edge of the boiling tub, holding his excess flesh in his hands. His body looked terrible this way, worse than it had when he was fat, and he marveled that Cherry had been able to stomach being with him at all. He looked like a thin man wearing an elephant suit, and though he took pride in his loss of weight, he now awaited the moment when his skin would respond. Where was its elasticity, where its renowned ability to bounce back?

He filled the wooden bucket with water and quickly poured it over his head, stinging himself into clarity with the heat. Was he going crazy, letting such thoughts as those last ones overtake him so? Cherry was gone, that was the truth of the matter, and even if she were injured why in the world would anyone call him? Nobody in Seoul even knew that they had been friends. It was ridiculous, and he was ridiculous too. Still, as Bobby sat there all alone and dismal, as he soaped his body and rubbed the calluses off the soles of his feet, all this time he mumbled to himself, "Not Cherry. Not Cherry. Please let it be someone else. . . ."

Bobby rinsed the soap from his back and stepped into the incredibly hot water and tried to sit down. As he sank slowly into it he could feel his pores opening, and he imagined bits of deep-down grime slowly floating up and leaving him clean. Underwater his body was like a fetus, and as he watched it turn redder he imagined his skin shrinking, saw himself stepping from the tub a new man.

Because it was late Bobby was surprised to hear the sounds of other bathers coming from the locker room. When the door opened and he looked through the steam, though, he realized that these men weren't naked but dressed. They waved their hands in front of their faces to help them see through the fog.

"Hello?" one of them said. "Ah, Mr. Bobby, we have found you." It was Mr. Soh and Headmaster Kim, wearing business suits. And as they began pulling up stools to sit down at the edge of the tub beside him Bobby thought, "Please, not Cherry."

"What's happened?" he asked. God, here they were all dressed up. This must be serious.

"You must help us," said Mr. Soh.

"Did you get a call from Seoul? Did somebody die?"

Mr. Soh chuckled. "Oh, we are sorry," he said. "Please don't worry. We had to say that to throw everyone away. Otherwise they would have been suspicious."

"Ah," Bobby said. "To throw everyone off."

The two men talked for a while in a dialect that Bobby couldn't understand. He felt wonderfully relieved but angry. What the hell kind of thing was that to do? Surely they hadn't meant it as a joke. Maybe it had something to do with Mr. Kwak and the Lees. . . .

"It's about spy-catching day," said Mr. Soh. "It has been put off until tomorrow. Do you remember Headmaster Kim's uncle? The man you met at the funeral shortly after you arrived?"

"Sure," said Bobby. " 'Love Potion Number Nine.' "

"Well, he was going to be our spy, but he's broken his foot and he suggested that you take his place.'

"Take his place doing what?" Bobby asked. "How did he break his foot?"

"Take his place as the spy, of course," said Mr. Soh. "An ox stepped on it."

This entire conversation had been in English and Mr. Soh had never sounded better. "Don't be silly," Bobby said. "The spy has to be Korean."

"Not at all," said Mr. Soh. "The spy could easily be foreign. And the Peace Corps would be the perfect ruse."

They were sitting there in their business suits, sweating like crazy and asking Bobby, who was naked under the water, to pretend to be a North Korean spy. And his best friends at the school were about to boycott the whole affair.

"No," he said. "I can't do it."

The headmaster and Mr. Soh spoke together again, purposefully using that heavy country dialect, and then they got off their stools and knelt down on the tiles, soaking their suits and bending their heads over and touching their noses to the floor.

"Headmaster Kim is deep in trouble," said Mr. Soh. "If we don't find a good spy tonight he will lose his job."

"Surely not," said Bobby. "After all, it's only a game."

"It is not a game," said Mr. Soh, practically hissing. "The Minister of Education—everyone is watching. This is the most important day for our course in moral education. You, from America, may find it hard to appreciate, but North Korean spies have landed at Taechon Beach before. And no one will suspect you. Everything will be fine."

"No," Bobby said. "Please. Surely you can find someone else. If I'm the spy everyone will say that you cheated."

He had expected the two men to confer again but they only knelt there, sad faces sweating, eyes down against the tiles. And to make matters worse, for the past several minutes Bobby had been dying to get out of the tub. His pores were as wide as barn doors by then, and he was feeling faint, his heart beating wildly around in his ears.

"I need to get out of the bath," he said.

"Must we ask again? Everything depends upon it."

"Oh, Christ," said Bobby, "alright. But you'll have to tell me what to do."

The two men stayed where they were, their foreheads down like that, embarrassing Bobby greatly and making him ask them once more to please get up.

"We'll go to your house and wait," said the headmaster, speaking to Bobby directly for the first time.

As soon as they were gone Bobby jumped from the tub and got cold water from the tap to pour across his desperate body. He dressed in his clean clothes and left the bath with dirty ones across his arm, looking up at the high half-moon and shaking his head at everything. Thirty minutes before, he had convinced himself that the Peace Corps was calling to tell him Cherry Consiliak was dead, and now he would be a North Korean spy. As he walked along he laughed, and his laugh caused a dog to bark, and that brought a couple of beggars back into the street.

I have been working on my speech for more than a fortnight now, and when I discovered that the American would not be around to hear it, I felt quite unhappy. Of course logic tells me that a man who has been studying Korean for less than a year cannot understand such a difficult speech, but I wanted him there just the same, pretending to understand as he stood by his chair.

Imagine my relief, then, when things changed and I was told that the American would be back in time to hear my speech after all. This speech represents ethical and moral education at its highest, and in past years it has been my finest moment. When I remind everyone that a society can exhibit good health only if the people of that society are knit together through a series of interdependent relationships, I can always see, in the shining of the teachers' eyes, that I have moved them by my words. It is the old values that come through in a speech like this, the old truths that are remembered—that is why I wanted the American to hear it. Think what it might mean if, through words of my own, the American actually began taking the world seriously for a change. If that were to happen I would retire a happy man. Think what it would mean to move the American. . . . That would be something to remember!

Written under a momentary clearing in the clouds as I try to understand whether or not it will rain.

4301年　　6月　　11日

Return

Six in the fourth place means: Walking in the midst of others, one returns alone.

The morning meeting was scheduled for eight and the students were assembled in the yard, waiting to be set loose upon the town. The students had rules too, of course. They could not detain anyone unless certain criteria were met. Overhearing someone ask the price of cigarettes was one of the criteria, as was a consensus concerning strangeness of dress or the genuinely odd nature of someone's speech.

Bobby had been told to wear odd clothing, so he found his oldest suit, a brown one bought at a Robert Hall store just before he went off to college. But since Bobby had been fat since high school, the suit fit loosely now, making him look, he thought, not so much like a spy as a fool.

All of the teachers stood when the vice-headmaster began his speech on the importance of moral education in a changing world, and when he finished Headmaster Kim came into the room. The headmaster was always pensive, but today he brought a soberness to his words that counteracted the general giddiness felt by the teachers at the prospect of a day of leisure, walking about the town.

"Last year," he said, "our spy was Mr. Nam's older brother who spent his day holed up inside the drugstore, getting captured late, just before the five o'clock deadline. It was a fine experience. The students worked together, which, we mustn't forget, is one of our goals, and everyone sharpened their ability to notice someone strange, someone odd, so that when the next real spy lands at Taechon Beach, he will not be able to walk among us with impunity, but will be found out quickly and brought into the hands of the authorities."

The headmaster's tone had the effect of dampening everyone's holiday mood and giving them a proper sense of gravity. Mr. Lee, when Bobby looked at him, was so grave that Bobby thought the floorboards beneath him might crack, but Mr. Kwak's face was quizzical, as if the headmaster had said something that had not occurred to him before.

"This year," continued Headmaster Kim, "we have confidence that our spy will not be caught. Of course, we secretly hope that he will be caught, but this year we have plumbed the depths of deception and come up with a wonderful spy, a foolproof spy. That is all I will say. The rules are known to you all, but I will reiterate that it is a teacher's job to interfere only if the students are bothering innocent people unnecessarily, or if you feel the real spy is at hand."

The teachers were stirring when the headmaster finished. In a moment they would release the students, who would stampede into the town like bulls into Pamplona. Could it be that Mr. Kwak and the Lees had foresworn their plan?

But as the headmaster sat down, the dissidents stepped away from their desks. Bobby could tell from the various faces around him that no one suspected a thing. And though he'd been sure that Mr. Kwak would do the talking it was Mr. Lee whose voice broke the general elation in the room.

"The three of us," he said, "would like to comment on spy-catching day and what we believe are its real implications for our society, for Koreans in general, and for our students here at Taechon Boys' Middle School."

Mr. Lee's tone was so quiet that the other teachers had not yet recognized it as contrary. The vice-headmaster, certainly, had not caught any of its underlying tone. His head moved mechanically, like a nodding dog in the back window of somebody's car.

"To be sure, North Korea sends out spies," Mr. Lee said, "but they are not everywhere and to search them out in this little yearly drama contributes to our students' already narrow view of the world, taking from them any hope of a democratic spirit and lessening Korea's already small opportunity to become a true democracy, where people are free to choose and to go about as they will."

By now, of course, everyone was alert, even the sleepers stirring like someone had just splashed water in their eyes. "What? What?" they said, and it was then that Mr. Kwak took over, making everyone turn his way.

"Therefore," he said, "Mr. Lee and Miss Lee and I respectfully decline to take part in spy-catching day. We will remain here, working on our lessons, and we urge any like-minded teachers to join us. We share with everyone a distaste for North Korea, so much so that we must protest activities that make us narrower and sillier in the eyes of the world, activities that contribute to our already well-developed inability to think for ourselves."

After Mr. Kwak spoke there was a moment of numbed silence, and then the place erupted.

"That's communist rhetoric!" shouted someone.

"Fools!" screamed someone else. "Inhuman fools!"

For a moment Bobby thought one of the teachers might

actually strike Mr. Kwak, but the place quieted again when Miss Lee insinuated her voice into the fray. It was the uncommonly high-pitched quality of the voice that got to them, coming across the top of all their protests like a siren.

"Friends! Friends!" she said. "When you think about it, spy-catching day is for fools. We need to build a country in which spies, when they come, will only want to stay, living freely among us, never to leave again."

This made a good number of the teachers laugh, whether because of what she'd said or because a woman was saying it, no one could be sure. But then all three of them sat back down, pretending to turn their attention to their lessons, while voices swirled around them like tornadoes, everyone aghast at the impropriety, the downright turncoat nature of it all.

Bobby didn't know how it would ever end, but through the limbs of the outraged faculty members he saw the headmaster rise from his chair and when that happened the others seemed to float back to theirs like so much driftwood after a storm.

"Teachers," said the headmaster, "I have one thing to say." He paused, letting everyone hear that there was no anger in his voice. He was looking not at the three traitors but over the heads of them all. Even Mr. Kwak took his eyes from his lesson book when the pause grew long. The headmaster made them wait, but in the end all he said was, "Everyone in this country is entitled to an opinion. Spy-catching day will, of course, go on as scheduled."

Then the vice-headmaster dismissed them, sending them out to the students and the warm June morning and the town where, everyone knew, a spy most certainly lurked. Bobby stood up and marched out too. And though he glanced back repeatedly, trying to catch the eye of one of his friends, they did not look up. They bent their heads to their lessons and were writing, fingers moving from text to paper as if they really were deciding what they would teach once they got their students back again.

Bobby did not know how to remove himself from the predicament he was in. It was clear as they marched that he should not have agreed to be the spy, but that had not been nearly so clear in the steam of the public bath, with Mr. Soh and Headmaster Kim burning their foreheads against the tiles. But where were his loyalties, where should they be? Mr. Kwak and the Lees were his true friends. They had shared the secret of their boycott as a sign of that friendship, and they were really standing up for courageous ideas in a country such as this, where open discussions about the North were out of the question. Freedom and democracy. Was he on their side, then, or on the other? He had been moved by their speeches, but to back away from his obligation to the headmaster after saying he'd do it seemed impossible.

All of this occurred to Bobby as he marched resolutely along in his oversized Robert Hall spy suit, among the disconcerted teachers and the happy students, who, anyone could see, viewed the whole thing as a lark.

When they got to the edge of town they spread out, students breaking into teams, teachers walking with their hands behind them, their gazes roaming. Bobby strolled for a while with Mr. Soh, but Mr. Soh said that the spy should act furtively, so he broke away and went into the market alone, examining the produce and looking for a place to buy cigarettes. Everyone knew he didn't smoke, so he recognized that this purchase was his one chance of being caught. And he really should have bought them early, he realized, for in the next instant the Goma found him.

"What's up?" asked the boy. "Has anybody spotted the spy yet?"

"Maybe this year they won't find him at all," Bobby said.

"Ha! You want to bet? We find him every year."

"You still owe me a thousand won," Bobby told him. "You should be thinking about paying me back, not betting."

"Double or nothing," said the Goma. "If I lose I'll pay tomorrow."

They argued for a while, but Bobby finally bet him, hoping to send him on his spy search so that he could go somewhere and quietly buy his cigarettes, first asking the price. Once that was accomplished he'd be home free.

Right then Mr. Nam came in from the other direction. Mr. Nam looked at the Goma in time to see him slip the old English book under his shirt.

"Hey!" said Nam. "I've been looking for that." He tried to grab him and the Goma backed away, running out of the market with Nam on his tail.

Bobby was near the Pusan-chip and would have bought the cigarettes there had the place been open. Way down here there were fewer students searching and he couldn't see any teachers on patrol, but there weren't any shops either, so he soon doubled back and came out in the center of things, where some students were questioning a farmer, asking his name and his place of origin. As he walked uptown he saw the Goma streak by, Mr. Nam behind him, and when he reached the tearoom he found that it was open again and went inside.

"Hello," he said. "Things are a mess out there."

"Ah," said Miss Moon.

Bobby sat near the door and Miss Moon stood by him, not even asking if he wanted coffee. The cigarettes were plainly visible on the counter and Bobby nodded in their direction. "So how much are they?" he asked.

"Why?" said Miss Moon. "You don't suppose the spy would be so stupid as to buy them here, do you?"

"No," Bobby said. "But when they were talking about it at school I realized that I didn't know the price either. I don't smoke, you know."

"I know that," she said, looking at him.

"So?" he asked.

"So what?"

"So how much are they?"

Miss Moon laughed, and right then the Goma came in. Bobby scowled. He couldn't even find out the price, let alone buy the things. He wondered if the rules required him to ask the price and buy the cigarettes at the same place, but he had no time to think. Here came the Goma, closing in.

"Any luck yet?" Bobby asked. "Any sign of the spy?"

The Goma was clearly frustrated, and he would have answered had Miss Moon not been laughing so hard. As it was, however, he just looked at her.

"What?" he asked. "What's so funny?"

Though Bobby knew Miss Moon had guessed he was the spy, he still had no idea she would give him away. But she stood up straight, pointed down at Bobby, and said, "It's him. He's the spy this year."

"Ha," said the Goma. "He can't be the spy, he's one of the teachers." But even as he spoke, his scab moved wider with his mouth. "Ho, ho," he said. "How do you know?"

"The cigarettes," said Miss Moon. "He wanted to know how much they were."

Did the spy have to admit it when he was caught? Certainly not to these two. Bobby was furious with Miss Moon and he said, "I only asked because I was curious. How the hell should I know what the stupid things cost?"

He frowned at them, but the Goma threw his head back like a colt.

"Ha!" he said. "Ha! Ha!"

"I am not the spy," said Bobby.

"Be right back," said the Goma, heading for the door.

He was going to sell the information. He would win the bet and sell the spy's identity to the students, just like he'd done in the past.

"This isn't fair!" Bobby said to Miss Moon. "You were supposed to be my friend!"

But she only looked at him strangely, then moved away a split second before the door flew open and the second-year students ran in. Mr. Pak, one of Bobby's favorites, was in the lead. "Did you ask the price of cigarettes?" he commanded.

"I didn't know how much they were," Bobby said. "I was only curious, it being such a big deal and all."

He realized then that he had never had a chance to survive the day uncaught. The whole town was geared up to inform on anyone.

"Are you," asked Mr. Pak, "a North Korean spy?"

"Take it easy," said Bobby. "It's only a game."

"Yes or no," Mr. Pak asked, raising his voice.

Korean students weren't supposed to speak to their teachers this way. Anyone else would have beat him for it.

"Yes," said Bobby. "Good job. You've caught me."

He thought the whole thing would end then, and he had just begun to worry about Mr. Kwak and the Lees again when all the students jumped him, throwing him out of his chair and pinning him to the floor, messing up his Robert Hall and giving him a rug burn too.

"Call the judges!" they yelled.

"Hey!" Bobby said. "Ouch! Hold it!"

But the students wouldn't let him speak, and once they had him pinned, a couple of them came forward with a rope.

"Tie him up quickly," said Mr. Pak. "Hooray for the second-year students. Hooray! Hooray!"

This was getting bad. Bobby hadn't thought he'd be caught and he certainly hadn't expected to be treated roughly if he were. He decided to be quiet until the judges arrived. Surely that would bring an end to it.

When the judges came, though, so did the rest of the student body, jamming the tearoom to its walls. Headmaster Kim, the main judge, had of course chosen Bobby, but he too looked at him harshly, as if trying to discern his true identity. After a moment of this examination he stood up and pronounced the second-year students the winners. They picked Bobby up and pulled him out the door. It appeared that he would now be the victim of a procession, all the way to school.

It was Mr. Pak's privilege to lead the spy up the street, but someone else quickly produced a sign that said, "Imbecilic North Korean spy dog," which was hung over Bobby's neck sandwich-board style. And as they moved along, everyone, all of the students, all of the Goma's entourage, and even passersby skipped and danced and sang, like extras in an extravaganza.

What followed once they got to school was a good many speeches. Everyone lined up in the yard, the headmaster presented the second-year students with a scroll, and Mr. Pak, on their behalf, challenged the other classes, vowing that his group would redouble their efforts, repeating the victory again when they were third-year kids.

Finally, things appeared to wind down. It was usually Judo Lee's job to call the students to the kind of smart attention necessary for dismissal, but Mr. Nam did that, barking at them until they were standing as straight as rods. Then they were gone, home free for the rest of the day.

After the students left, the teachers came around to congratulate Bobby, and the headmaster himself opened a little pocketknife and cut his ropes away. Mr. Soh loaned

Bobby a comb, and even Mr. Nam, who had spent the whole day in pursuit of the Goma, smiled and shook his hand.

In other years there had been pots of makkoli in the teachers' room, and after the successful completion of spy-catching day the teachers had all gotten drunk. This day, however, though the makkoli pots were full, everyone reentered the room cautiously. To be sure, some of the teachers would have immediately become as rowdy as possible, but most of them were quiet and surprisingly circumspect, walking past the dissidents on tiptoe, then rolling their chairs over to the unlit stove.

Bobby's desk, of course, was right in the middle of the action, but he was not about to move away. He sat down and looked straight at Mr. Kwak. "I was the spy," he said. "You probably noticed that."

When Bobby finished speaking, Mr. Kwak immediately smiled, looking at him ironically, and Miss Lee did too. Only Judo Lee continued looking down.

"I'm sorry," Bobby said. "It was a special request of the headmaster and I could not find any way to refuse. It was a last-minute thing, an emergency."

Mr. Kwak nodded. "These things happen," he said. "Our loyalties are constantly at risk."

Bobby was feeling terrible, but before he could speak again the school secretary came in and said that the head-master wanted to see the Lees and Mr. Kwak in his office. Her voice carried none of the weight of the announce-ment, but when the three stood up, the effect on the room was tremendous. Mr. Lee led the way, never looking back, and the others marched behind him, their dignity contained in the crispness of their step.

Bobby put his head on his arms, across the place on his wrists where the ropes had burned his skin. It was hopeless, he thought. He had done the wrong thing, realizing it, as usual, too late. When would he learn to stand up for his beliefs, to do the right thing? His friends were in the principal's office, and this idiot Nam was standing above him, waiting for an opportunity to speak. He might have stayed there for hours, but when someone tapped him on the shoulder he looked up into the kindly eyes of the vice-headmaster, the moral leader of the school. He had carried a full bowl of makkoli across the room and was trying not to spill any of it as he waited for Bobby to take it from his hands.

The day went on forever. The entire week did. On the way home from school a few people nodded to Bobby, saying what a good job he'd done as spy, and when he left Policeman Kim's house again, he discovered everyone was talking about it, and he knew his place in the town had been enhanced by what he had done. His immediate problem, however, was this: today he had his judo lesson and he had betrayed the toughest man in town, and the very one who would, if he showed up, now have an opportunity to pound him mercilessly, all in the name of sport. Of course, Bobby didn't think that Mr. Lee would show up, but for him to stay away was impossible. So at a little after five, with his judo gear under his arm, he walked into the gym. Judo Lee was already dressed and waiting, preparing, Bobby feared, to teach him the lesson of his life.

"Change your clothes," said Lee, whose center of gravity right then seemed about two feet off the ground.

"I didn't think you'd come," said Bobby. "I'm very sorry about everything."

"You're late. Change quickly."

There was no changing room in the practice hall, so Bobby turned his back, stepped feebly out of his clothing, and then wrapped the heavy judo-bok around him, his white belt tied at the middle like a handle. Mr. Lee was waiting in the center of the mat, and he bowed and advanced quickly, his hands held like a gunfighter's but his eyes vacant, focusing, Bobby was sure, on his betrayal earlier in the day.

"Balance is everything," said Mr. Lee, sweeping Bobby's ankle away and letting him fall down on his side. "In judo you should never commit yourself."

Bobby stood again and Judo Lee came in with an ankle sweep on the other side. Bobby countered nicely by leaving his feet altogether, jumping up into the air.

"Move laterally," said Mr. Lee. "Don't jump around so."

He pulled Bobby into a right hip roll, and when Bobby countered he changed direction instantly and sent him sailing, feet up by the ceiling, head down over the mat. But Mr. Lee didn't let go of Bobby's clothing, and when he hit he was horizontal again and slapped the mat with his left arm and side, just like he'd been taught to do.

"Good fall," said Judo Lee. "It is necessary to learn to take defeat well."

Mr. Lee was tough, but Bobby was five years younger, so the next time Mr. Lee came at him Bobby spun hard to his right, coming up behind Mr. Lee and grabbing him in a bear hug. Both of Mr. Lee's arms were inside his grasp.

"Ha," Bobby said, lifting his opponent off the ground.

"Ha, yourself," said Judo Lee. The moment Bobby pulled, he jumped, throwing himself up over Bobby's head, breaking Bobby's grip and landing on his feet behind him, just like the hero in a Chinese movie. Judo Lee reached down and grabbed both Bobby's ankles, pulling them away and letting him crush his face into the floor.

"None of this is any good," he said. "You are not staying low, and you have not yet learned where you are supposed to be."

When Bobby stood he had a bloody nose, but the lesson

went on. They moved into the knife defense, Mr. Lee
forcing Bobby's arms just to the breaking point before
releasing them unharmed. "Like this," he said again and
again. And when the lesson ended an hour later, they
were both lying on the mat, Bobby exhausted to the point
of nausea but Judo Lee tired too, sweat dripping from his
big round face.

It was their usual custom to repair to the tearoom after
their lessons. Mr. Lee wouldn't take money for what he
taught, so Bobby bought the tea and they generally sat
quietly, idly watching Miss Moon and resting. Today,
however, Bobby was shy about mentioning the tearoom,
and if Mr. Lee had not lingered at the door, he would
have gone home alone, humbled somehow by still being
in one piece.

Mr. Lee did wait for him, though, and as they walked
up the street he said, "Miss Lee and I were simple. Kwak
was too."

Bobby wasn't sure what he meant by "simple," so he
waited, hoping for a little expansion and also a clue as to
just how badly he had fared in the eyes of this excellent
man.

"Headmaster Kim, though, is not simple," Mr Lee continued. "He will let the Ministry deal with me and Miss
Lee, but he fired Kwak immediately, right after school."

"He can't do that!" Bobby said, surprised and truly
indignant. "Mr. Kwak's the best English teacher he's got!"

"Sure," said Judo Lee. "But Kwak was hired here. So
he can be fired here too."

They didn't speak again, but when they got to the
tearoom they discovered that it was closed. And this time
not only were the lights out, but the sign was down.

Bobby wanted to talk more about Mr. Kwak, but Judo
Lee brushed his concern aside. He rattled the tearoom

door, then threw up his hands. "I'm not in the mood for tea anyway," he said. "Tonight let's drink. Come, I know a place where you have never been."

Bobby wanted to know what had happened to Miss Moon, but he quickly followed Mr. Lee off into the night, walking down an unfamiliar road to the Moon-Hwa-chip, the fanciest bar in town. Before they got there, however, the Goma came out of an alley and fell in behind them. He was carrying something and was acting unusually subdued, and Bobby remembered that the Goma had been the one to turn him in to the students. What the hell, he thought, why not let the Goma profit from this awful day?

When they stepped into the lighted circle made by the Moon-hwa-chip's electric sign, Bobby saw that the Goma was carrying a sack of oranges, big ones in a thin string bag.

"These are for you," the Goma said.

He handed Bobby the bag, which weighed at least twenty pounds. No one had broken the seal since it had been packed in California. These were American oranges. It was a terrific gift.

"Where did these come from?" Bobby asked, but Mr. Lee, who was looking at the oranges too, wasn't asking any questions. "Never mind," he said. "Let's have one."

So they sat down on the steps of the bar, and Bobby pulled the strings apart and handed oranges all around. When Mr. Lee dug his thumbnail through the outer skin of his orange a line of juice came up and hit Bobby in the eye.

"These are good," said Judo Lee. He pulled out a couple of bank notes and pointed at a candlelit shack across the street. "Ah, Goma," he said, "run over there and buy us some *soju*," and the Goma was gone in a flash, everyone's servant, hurrying to bring them back a bottle of the acid drink.

By the time the Goma returned, Bobby had started his second orange and Mr. Lee his third. They were wonderful, juicy and full and sweet. And when Mr. Lee popped the cap on the *soju*, they drank as they ate, listening to the faint sounds of women talking inside the bar.

Mr. Lee and Bobby ate and drank for another half hour without saying a word, until the bar's door opened and some early customers came out, walking down the steps and past them into the night.

"Good-bye!" the bar hostesses called. Then they waited until the customers were out of sight before looking down.

"Oh," they said. "Good evening, gentlemen. Are you coming inside?"

It was such a clear night, the moon hovering high above the bar, that Bobby hoped Mr. Lee might say that they were not. But to his surprise Mr. Lee didn't answer. Rather, as if he had not seen the customers or heard the greeting, Mr. Lee began to sing. He had an orange peel in his hand, and he looked up at the moon and sang a song that made Bobby feel even sadder than he had before. Bobby couldn't understand the lyrics, but one of the women stepped down from the doorway and was soon singing along with Mr. Lee, her voice winding around his like a delicate vine.

Finally Mr. Lee shook himself free of his melancholy and smiled at his singing partner.

"Yes," he said, in answer to the woman's question of a long moment before. He took Bobby's arm and shook it slightly. "Yes," he said, "we are coming inside."

Ah, I am a man of profound intuition! I knew all along that there was something about our American that did not meet the eye, but until today I had no proof with which to justify my belief.

But today, today I was so proud! Imagine, unbeknownst to everyone, and in the face of all that silliness from Mr. Kwak and Mr. Lee, our American agreed to be the spy! And he succeeded beautifully, looking spylike and strange, and pretending to be irritated when he was caught. What an actor, what a commendable man!

I must admit, though I disagree with the headmaster on many things, choosing Mr. Bobby as the spy was a stroke of genius, and though I know he only agreed to do it out of loyalty to the school, another good thing to come of it is that Mr. Nam will now have to shut up, no longer calling the man a liar. "One man's lie is another man's joke," I told Mr. Nam, but I wish now that I had not waited until today to say it.

After the spy-catching-day formalities ended, I made my first move toward the friendship that I now know will come to exist between Mr. Bobby and me. He was tired and dozing at his desk, so I took him a bowl of makkoli and smiled, thus clearing the way for our relationship—younger brother, older brother— to begin. And I am now looking forward to him making the next move.

Imagine how much I have learned in this, my last year as the vice-headmaster of our school. I have learned that the world is large, but that the five relationships can encompass it all. I have learned that strangeness of face dims with time, and that fat can fall away from a man's bones like the shell from a nut.

Oh, I am a happy man today!

Written at my desk, late in the evening, as I look around at the dim, empty teachers' room and imagine myself retired.

4301 年　6 月　12 日

Part Three

Following

=== ===
=== ===

*Nine at the beginning means: To go out the door
in company produces deeds.*

The events of the days surrounding Bobby's betrayal of his Korean friends had so overwhelmed Bobby that when summer vacation finally came he didn't travel as he'd thought he would, but simply stayed in town for a long, quiet rest.

During the final weeks of school he led a circumspect life, stacking his books over onto Mr. Kwak's empty desk, but otherwise ignoring Mr. Kwak's departure as completely as he could. Mr. Lee and Miss Lee would be transferred too, everyone said, but while they were still around, Bobby maintained a respectful distance: that of a contrite friend awaiting acceptance once again. Mr. Lee understood his intentions and continued throwing him good-naturedly around the gym. Miss Lee too smiled at him, though she did no more than that.

In September Bobby began to feel run down. His mammoth weight loss had until then given him only cause for joy. Now, though, when the grandmother stopped by his

159

room, Bobby occasionally joined her in her coughing fits. And if he exerted himself too much, his lungs felt sore. By November he was forced to give up judo, and in December he made arrangements to travel to Seoul, where there was a Peace Corps doctor, to find out what was wrong.

On the evening before his departure, Bobby stopped by the Pusan-chip to pay his tab. It should be noted that Miss Kim, the girl who had worked in the Pusan-chip when Bobby arrived in town, had moved away to marry a farmer's son and that during the fall and early winter the owner had been running the place alone. All the regular customers hoped that she would find a helper soon, and a common subject of discussion was whether Miss Kim's eventual replacement would be prettier or uglier, whether she would have a good singing voice or a bad one, and whether she would have a good sense of humor. Miss Kim, everyone agreed, had been wonderful and they were lucky to have had her for so long.

So when Bobby opened the door that night, he was surprised to find that Miss Kim's replacement was at hand, and that she was none other than Miss Moon. He had been going by the tearoom periodically ever since spy-catching day, but it had not reopened, and no one had been able to tell him why.

The bar was empty, except for Miss Moon, the owner, and the Goma, who sat in the corner staring at his English book.

"My God, Miss Moon," said Bobby.

"Close the door," said the Goma.

The owner greeted Bobby in her usual way, and Miss Moon bowed slightly before turning to the makkoli pots and preparing to bring him a drink.

"I believe you know our new girl," said the owner.

It was the owner's habit, early each evening, to visit other nearby bars in order to chat and gossip for a while, but tonight she had a stew on the fire and could not leave until it was done. Bobby therefore looked around at the Goma, sensing that he should not focus too much attention on Miss Moon. The Goma had been avoiding Mr. Nam for months by then, and he was never without his English book. For all Bobby knew, he really had been studying the thing. When the Goma saw Bobby looking at him, he smiled.

"Can you really read that book?" Bobby asked.

"You bet," said the Goma.

Miss Moon, whose job was to entertain, came over and sat down. Bobby noticed a tragic air about her, but since the owner's eyes were on them, he continued talking to the Goma while trying to read something in Miss Moon's downcast eyes.

"Do you know what the words mean?" he asked. "Do you know what the meaning is of the things you say?"

"Sure," said the Goma, "Enough's as good as a feast."

Bobby hadn't seen the Goma in weeks, but for him to actually learn anything from Mr. Nam's book seemed impossible. Bobby didn't think he could even read Korean well.

"What if I spoke to you in English?" Bobby asked. "Would you understand?"

"Beats me," the Goma said.

Bobby turned on his stool and, switching to his native tongue, said, "How are you today, Goma? Are you feeling fine?" He knew the question, in just that form, was right out of Mr. Nam's book, and he waited for the Goma to give him the book's response.

"Cool as a cucumber," the Goma said.

"Isn't it wonderful how the weather has cleared?"

"Yessiree, Bob. Not a cloud in the sky."

Bobby paused, trying to remember what else was in the book. Those two questions had been on the first page, but he did know one line from somewhere farther back.

"How about it, Mack?" he said. "Lend me a sawbuck till Saturday night."

"Not a chance, pal," said the Goma. "You're barking up the wrong tree."

It was incredible but it appeared that the Goma really had memorized Mr. Nam's entire book, questions and answers both.

"This is wonderful, Goma," said Bobby, speaking Korean again. "You should be proud."

"Piece of cake," said he. "Like taking candy from a baby."

By this time the owner's stew was sufficiently cooked so she slipped into her overcoat, telling Miss Moon she wouldn't be a minute, that she only wanted to say hello to a friend. And the moment the door closed, Miss Moon began to cry.

"You will want something more to drink," she said.

"You just disappeared," said Bobby. "You didn't even say good-bye."

He had worried, since she was already crying, that his comment might make her cry harder, but instead she stiffened, standing and going back by the makkoli pots.

"That tearoom was always losing money," she said. "Did you expect it to stay open on your thirty won a day?"

"No," said Bobby. "But we were friends. And you left so abruptly."

He was completely at a loss. Miss Moon seemed so different now. She was thinner and her face carried its more tragic lines so forthrightly.

"Come," she said. "Buy another bowl of wine. I am here to drink with you."

Miss Moon filled Bobby's bowl, though he had barely touched it, and poured a large one for herself. "How about that little twerp?" she asked, pointing at the Goma.

Bobby was taken aback. Miss Moon had always been unfailingly kind to the Goma.

"Sure," Bobby said. "If he wants a drink let's give him one."

But when she called his name, even the Goma came on careful feet, seeing the change in her and on his guard for some trick. Would she throw the bowl of makkoli in his face, perhaps? Everyone was mean to the Goma. Until now Miss Moon had been a rare exception.

Some ten minutes went by without anyone speaking. The Goma turned his back so that if she did take a swipe at him he'd be able to dodge, but Miss Moon was content to gulp what she had poured for herself and then shove her bowl across the bar. But as the silence continued Bobby did observe that some of Miss Moon's old facial qualities were beginning to return. There, in the corners of her eyes, was the softness that she used to exhibit when listening to the Love Tearoom's serious songs. There, where the smooth skin of her chin began its gentle descent, was a tremor so slight that it spoke volumes, as if it were the hiding place of her real and former self.

But they really didn't talk at all. And when the owner came back she was followed by some of the regular customers, and by Mr. Soh, who had been looking everywhere for Bobby.

"Ah," he said. "Headmaster Kim is having a party and he hoped that I would be able to bring you along."

"What? You mean right now?"

"Yes," he said. "The vice-headmaster's retirement is near."

Bobby looked around the bar a moment but then stood to go with Mr. Soh. Since it was early he promised himself that he'd leave the headmaster's party before curfew, and come back down here later to find out what was really going on.

"You realize," said Mr. Soh, "that I'm talking about a party at Headmaster Kim's house. A thing like that doesn't happen every day."

Headmaster Kim had a substantial house, built like Policeman Kim's but larger and better appointed. The teachers were gathered in the living room, around a low table, the vice-headmaster at one end, the headmaster at the other. When he and Mr. Soh walked in, everyone moved around to make room for them. Bobby looked for Mr. Nam and then sat down away from him, up next to the vice-headmaster, of whom he had recently grown fond. There were many bottles of scotch on the table and mountains of food.

"What a glorious time we are having and how wonderful that you have come!" said the vice-headmaster. "Soon I shall retire, but I will always remember this day!" He grabbed a glass and poured it half full of warm scotch, splashing it at Bobby.

"I would like to propose a toast," said Headmaster Kim. "To our vice-headmaster, who has been in the business of educating boys for thirty years."

Everyone held their glasses high while the vice-headmaster bobbed his head in thanks. For his part, Bobby lowered his glass until the brim of it was below the table's edge. Then he quietly placed it on the floor. Unfortunately the vice-headmaster saw him and was very quick to lower his own glass, pouring part of its contents into Bobby's.

"Ha ha," he said. Then he lifted his glass up until Bobby was forced to pull his full one back off the floor. *"Mani Tushipsho,"* said the vice-headmaster. "To your continued good health."

Bobby had had a bowl of makkoli at the Pusan-chip and he'd put the scotch to his lips once or twice here, but with the vice-headmaster staring at him, challenge all over his face, he could think of nothing to do but stand up and ask where the toilet was, taking his whiskey with him when he left the room. Ill or not, pouring booze away while pretending not to was, after all, as Korean as apple pie.

It was freezing outside. Bobby had not brought his coat and the outhouse shoes were so small that he could barely walk in them. But there was a clear moon above him and as he walked he looked ahead, hoping to find another moon cut into the outhouse door. Instead he saw the Goma standing there. "Hail fellow well met," he said.

"Hey," said Bobby, "where have you been?"

The Goma pointed to a sand pit at the side of the house, just under the window where the vice-headmaster sat.

"It's a good place to listen," he said.

When Bobby offered him a sip of scotch he downed half of it in a gulp, holding on tight while it warmed his insides.

"Holy cow!" he said.

Bobby left the Goma with his whiskey glass while he stepped into the outhouse, and when he came back out the Goma was gone. Alas, though he'd solved the problem of the whiskey, he had lost the glass as well. And there was Mr. Nam, standing on the doorstep, waiting his turn.

"If I had the nerve I would leave now," said Mr. Nam. "From this point forward all Korean parties go downhill." He looked at his watch and shook his head. "It's still early, no one will be allowed to go home until eleven."

Mr. Nam hovered there with Bobby for a moment, but when he heard someone else coming out he hurried on. Bobby watched him go and then looked toward the side of the house where the Goma was standing. He threw Bobby the empty glass and then darted away just as another man appeared, full whiskey glass in hand.

For the next hour, once everyone was back inside, the

staff of Taechon Boys' Middle School took it easy on drink and dedicated itself to song. Bobby sang "The Bald-Headed Bachelor," and the vice-headmaster sang "O Solo Mio" reasonably well. After much coaxing the headmaster took a couple of toothpicks, used them to prop his eyes wide open, and then did a Chinese dragon dance all around the room. It was fun, and though Bobby was tired, he was pleased to be taken for granted, accepted as one of the teachers, his specialness slipping ever so steadily away.

At eleven o'clock they all sang the vice-headmaster's favorite song, "Auld Lang Syne," with Mr. Nam asking Bobby whether its proper English title was "The Good Old Times" or "The Old Good Times." And when the party ended and they all walked out together, the vice-headmaster was by Bobby's side. "I've got two wives," he said. "I'm the only one at school with two wives."

For a moment Headmaster Kim stood waving to them from the edge of his garden. His one wife was by his side, and a few children and old people had come from the house to bid them farewell. By the time they got to the main street, teachers were staggering everywhere, lurching to and fro, but though Bobby expected to have trouble getting away from them, he did not. All he had to do was bob and weave like they did for a while, then duck into the shadows and wait for the last of the teachers to stumble off toward home. And when the street was clear he buttoned his jacket and walked back down toward the Pusan-chip to find out what was really going on.

Of course, he was not alone. As he walked, the Goma slid from the shadows and matched him stride for stride, like Wyatt Earp and his deputy heading for the OK Corral.

When they got to the Pusan-chip the light was off, but they slid back the door anyway. They stepped into a scene of chaos. The customers were gone, but the stools in the front room were turned on their sides, one of them broken, and makkoli bowls were everywhere. The owner was hunched over the fire, her knees wide, staring into the great valley of her skirt. She hardly looked up when they came in.

Looking around, Bobby noticed that someone had shoved a makkoli bowl through the paper of the backroom door, so now there was a hole the size of a big man's head, low down and off to one side. When Bobby looked through the hole he could see the sleeping figure of a farmer, but nothing of Miss Moon. The whole place was drenched in makkoli. Even the Goma, who had spent his evening in a sand pit, stepped lightly and seemed offended by the lavish destruction.

They opened the door and stepped into the back room and tiptoed across the stains. The farmer was soaked and out cold, but he was alive. And when Bobby turned around, he found Miss Moon huddled in the corner, her gown in shreds, one bare knee up under her chin.

"Sure is a sight for sore eyes," said the Goma.

Bobby had spent a good deal of time at the Pusan-chip, and the wreckage was more than just the results of another evening at play. Miss Moon didn't seem injured, but though Bobby shook her shoulders he couldn't get her to respond.

"She's dead," said the Goma.

They stepped back down into the main room again and tried their luck with the owner.

"What happened here? Was anyone hurt?"

The owner shook her head. "It will take me all night to clean up," she said. "How about giving a hand?"

Though ruined, the Pusan-chip was small, and when the owner began to stir, Bobby and the Goma set about putting things right. They cleaned up the broken furniture, sat the stools back up, and stacked all the bowls. The owner had a tub of soapy water, and the Goma went behind the bar once the bowls were collected and began washing them. Bobby found a mop and attacked the pools of makkoli on the back room floor while the owner made tea. It didn't take long and the work made them all feel better.

Once the tea was ready, the owner went out and came back quickly with a blanket for the farmer and a dry change of clothes for Miss Moon, who was beginning to wobble a bit. When the clothes were presented to her she changed into them all by herself in the corner.

When the tea was poured and they had stools to sit on, and when Miss Moon was propped in the doorway with her hands wrapped around a warm cup of the stuff, the owner told them what had happened.

"That gent back there," she said, jerking a thumb toward the other room, "claims he owns this girl. He's a bumpkin, but he has a big farm and he claims some men talked him into putting all his money into that tearoom that went broke. He lost everything and says they gave him this girl as compensation for his loss. He's had her out there on his farm since then, but a week ago she took off, coming back here. I let him drink on the house and finally the other farmers tried to dislodge him, but he stood up to us all. When he wakes up he'll start haranguing again. I took her on to help her, but one night of this is enough."

Bobby looked at the Goma. The owner's accent was so countrified that Bobby wasn't sure he had it right. But the Goma nodded. "It's got the ring of truth to it," he said.

"Why doesn't she go to the police?" Bobby asked, but the Goma and the owner both looked at him like his question should not be dignified with a response. At that moment Miss Moon stepped down into the main room and put her hand on Bobby's shoulder.

"It's all true," she said. "What I need now is money so that I can run away."

Bobby looked at the owner, but she shrugged. She had done all she was going to, just by giving Miss Moon the job.

"How much do you need?" he asked. "Where will you go?"

"Anywhere," she said. "But now, before he wakes up."

The clothes that the owner had brought for Miss Moon were men's, and as Bobby looked at them the thought crossed his mind that maybe he was being played for a fool. Maybe the farmer had nothing to do with Miss Moon and the object of the whole story was money. But surely not. If anyone did, the owner of this bar knew that he was nearly always broke. Bobby did have the money he was going to use to pay his tab, and he told the Goma to take Miss Moon back to his inn and to hide her there until the morning train left for Seoul. By then it was nearly midnight and since the train left early, Bobby wanted to go back home for a few hours' sleep. The owner, however, seemed to think that they would sit a while longer, warming their hands on the cups. She was in need of a bar girl again but she didn't seem to mind.

"There is always an abundance of pretty young girls," she said. "The trick is finding one who will work."

Bobby sat there until the owner saw that he was tired. He then took the blanket she offered him and went in to lay down next to the farmer for a while.

It wasn't the curfew that kept him from going home, but his lack of energy for the walk.

The Family

☰ ☲

Six in the second place means: She should not follow her whims.

It took Bobby and Miss Moon eight hours to get to Seoul, though the trip on the fast train would have taken four. Their departure was uneventful. The Goma was there, but the Pusan-chip's madam had taken the farmer by the arm and helped him with a house-by-house search of the farthest reaches of the town.

Bobby couldn't believe the size of Seoul. Though he remembered little of it from the days he'd spent there, he knew it hadn't seemed nearly as large then as it did now. Since neither of them had the courage to face a bus ride, they spent his remaining money and took a cab.

There was an inn across the street from the Peace Corps office, and luckily the first person they asked pointed it out. This was a cheap home for out-of-town volunteers, a place where they could exchange gossip and speak American English into the small hours of the night.

Though they'd spent some of the train ride trying to catch up on their sleep, the farther they got from Taechon, the more apparent it became to Bobby that the Miss Moon riding along with him was the tearoom Miss Moon of old. Even as she slept, he could see a softer version of her returning, casting the harsher one out mile by mile.

"I'm sorry," Bobby said. "But we can't afford two rooms."

Miss Moon took his arm. "Never mind," she told him. "I still remember my promise."

He remembered her promise too—that someday they would be together. She had told him that as she'd pushed him from the tearoom door, sending him home to defecate in his room. Bobby had recognized even then that it was a common promise made to drunken passersby, and he felt sorry that she felt she had to bring it up now.

When they got to the inn the owner greeted them strangely. There was only one room left, she said, a small one renting for four hundred won a night.

"The Peace Corps office will open in the morning," said Bobby. "Surely you understand that I am good for it."

"Of course," said the owner after a pause.

Just then Bobby realized that Miss Moon was still wearing her odd assortment of clothing, and he understood that the owner's reticence was due as much to Miss Moon's strangeness as to his lack of funds. Peace Corps volunteers usually came alone. To bring a Korean girl in was passably common during the later hours, but such an early, sober-headed entrance was unusual. Nevertheless, they were shortly shown to their room and allowed to collapse there, barely pulling the bedding from the shelves before falling down on it to nap.

Some Peace Corps volunteers came to Seoul often, some did not. And those who did not were looked upon with a mixture of awe and suspicion by those who did. Bobby, for example, had not seen a single member of his group other than Cherry and Larry Corsio since their arrival fifteen months before. So when, early that evening, he

awoke and stepped out to ask where he and Miss Moon
might find a cheap place to eat, his presence was greeted
with shocked surprise by the three young men who happened to be standing in the hall.

"Who's that?" said someone named Mac. "My God,
man, you've shrunk!"

"Hey," said Bobby, pleased. "How's everybody?"

The three had all been in his training group, all solo
volunteers like himself living in the provinces, and up to
Seoul for a week or two of winter fun.

"We thought you died," said a volunteer named Allen,
and the third, whose name was Robert, rushed over to
shake his hand. They all started to smile and chuckle, as
Bobby remembered doing at the missile base with Cherry.
Though he hadn't known these guys well, he was terribly
glad to see them, especially since they were shocked at
his diminished size.

"Come out with us," said Mac. "We're about to head
into Itewon, see how the other half lives."

Itewon housed Seoul's version of the Vil, a huge strip
of bars and clubs near the main U.S. military base.

"I can imagine how they live," Bobby said. "I've got
someone with me, and I'm broke."

"I'm loaded," said Mac, but then he paused. "What do
you mean? Who do you have with you?"

Bobby explained about Miss Moon, telling them about
the closure of the tearoom, the narrow escape from the
farmer at the Pusan-chip the night before.

"Good God," said Robert. "I thought you'd been
spending all your time studying."

They stood talking, putting off deciding what to do that
evening, until they heard Miss Moon moving around inside the room. "I'll tell you what," said Mac. "Take us
in and introduce us. Who knows? Maybe she'll fit in."

Of the three, Allen was the most formal, but they all
spoke to Miss Moon politely, and all in good Korean.

Robert, the most diligent student, carried a shoulder bag of dictionaries with him, but Mac was the most colloquial, speaking to Miss Moon like an equal, just as Bobby had done back in the tearoom days, when everything was simple and clear. In return Miss Moon was far less guarded with the three strangers than Bobby had expected. Indeed, she seemed delighted. She was well rested from the trip and her cheerfulness had completely returned.

When Bobby, after nearly an hour of altogether pleasant chatter, said that he wanted to eat, Robert pulled a can of army peanut butter and C-ration crackers from his dictionary bag and Allen laid a pack of cigarettes on the floor. "In that case maybe we'd better smoke a joint," he said, and he nodded toward Miss Moon as if asking Bobby's permission.

Bobby didn't know what Miss Moon would think about the joint, and he was really more interested in the peanut butter, so Allen struck a match, and just as the first of the crackers was spread, the joint came by. Bobby had often wondered, during his months alone, what the difference was between acting the part of a conservative man in the world and acting the part of a liberal one. What did those words mean? This joint, as an example, sticking to his fingers and sending little alterations into his bloodstream, was it serious business? Or was it just another means of passing time, a good way of making army peanut butter taste wondrously good? He really had no idea. Still, he passed the joint on to Mac and ate three of the crackers straight away. And when the joint got to Miss Moon she dug down in her bag, laying a pack of cigarettes on the floor. "Please," she said, "no need to share. Have one of mine."

When they left the inn it was eight o'clock and they'd all pretty much resigned themselves to letting Mac spend his money on taking them out for the night. As they hailed a taxi and all climbed in, Miss Moon was happy as a lark, chirping away. She was free of the farmer and free of the Love tearoom with all its saxophone-dominated songs, of dimly lit days and nights of murderous repetition. She had discovered an unexpected opportunity and would take advantage of it if she could, of that there was no question.

Arriving at Itewon was like coming into Las Vegas after months on the surrounding desert, a sensation that heightened the sparkle in Miss Moon's eyes and made Bobby's friends leap from the cab in order to form a corridor down which she could walk. Above them and along the strip there were neon cowboys and flashing dice and strolling hoards of GIs and Korean girls and hawkers and transvestites and pimps.

"Isn't this great?" said Mac. "What did I tell you?"

"It's obscene," said Robert, but he swung his dictionary bag easily and seemed expansive in the chilly air.

Robert and Mac walked ahead but Allen stayed back with Bobby and Miss Moon. It was clear that without her presence he would have been satisfied to stay in the inn and smoke.

"Now what?" he said to Mac. "Just walking into one of these places has got to cost a bundle."

But Mac patted the pocket of his worn-out corduroy coat and put a finger to his lips.

"If we get separated we'll reconnoiter here," he said. He spoke like a platoon leader, in contrast to his long hair that was pulled straight back from his forehead and fell down his back like Beethoven's. His was a military approach to carousing.

"Remember, Mac," said Allen. "You're the one with money. Stay with us or give us our share now."

Since there were crowds all along the street, Bobby had expected that Miss Moon would take his arm, but she seemed captivated and completely unafraid. And though he had trouble believing it, the bar Mar chose for them was called the Lucky Seven Club, where the lights were low and the music was psychedelic.

"Christ, man, you're not taking her in there, are you?" said Allen. "She just got into town." Mac was far enough through the door not to hear, though, and Miss Moon was oblivious to Allen's protectiveness.

Once inside the bar it became obvious that finding a place to sit was going to be impossible, and Bobby was beginning to agree with Allen—why not just get something to eat and then go on back to the inn to sleep? This was the military's world and they didn't belong here. Suddenly, however, someone pulled on his arm and he turned to see another American staring at him. The man was wearing jeans and a sweater and it took Bobby a moment to realize that this was Ron, Gary Smith's buddy, in whose hooch he'd slept the night that Cherry left town.

"Bobby, I can't believe you're here." Ron nodded off toward the corner of the bar where he and some friends had a table. "Come. Please. Join us," he said.

It was noisy in the bar but when they got to the table people squeezed together. Ron was with three other military guys, none of whose names Bobby caught.

Miss Moon took a seat at the head of the table, between Ron and Bobby, and when Bobby told everyone that they'd only come to Seoul that day and that Miss Moon had never been there before, they all became gentlemen, each trying to outdo the other. But something else happened when they sat down as well. A certain line of contact, a certain channel, seemed to have opened up between Miss Moon and Ron, though as with Ron and Miss Kim so many months before, they had no common language.

"He has wonderful-looking skin, doesn't he?" Miss Moon told Bobby. "Ask him what he does to make it so smooth."

Bobby was embarrassed by the question, but Miss Moon insisted.

"What?" said Ron.

"She wants to know about your skin. . . . How you keep it looking so smooth."

Ron gave Bobby a long look, but in a moment he took Miss Moon's arm, pulled her sleeve back to her elbow, and laid his own arm down next to hers. "Look," he said. "Don't they make a nice match?"

Ron and his friends were celebrating the departure of one of them for home the next day, and they wouldn't let Mac pay for anything. They ordered beer and told the waiter to bring chips and peanuts and cheese. The friend who was leaving seemed shaken by the fact, and was determined to go out smashed. Ron, however, immediately became involved in an eyes-only conversation with Miss Moon, and after a while the two groups went back to talking among themselves. Allen wasn't much of a drinker, and now that Miss Moon was out of his domain he wanted to go out and find a place to light another joint. Mac and Robert kept watching all the Korean girls, commenting on them as they moved in and out of the circles of light.

"Now that we've got a home base," said Mac, "how about taking a little stroll, stretch the old legs a bit?"

As soon as he spoke, Robert was ready and Allen, too, saw this as his chance for another smoke. Bobby was reluctant to go with them, but Ron had heard and prompted him.

"You go on," he said. "I'll take care of Miss Moon." And when Bobby told her what they were thinking of doing she mimicked Ron's tone exactly. "Please go," she said. "I've got to learn to take care of myself sometime. It might as well be now."

So when his three friends finished their beers, they all

got up, Robert tucking his dictionary bag under the table when Ron told him it would be safe.

The question now was whether they would take their walk inside the bar or out. Allen wanted to lead everyone toward the door, but Robert was immediately waylaid by a pretty young girl and Mac was looking around to see if she had a friend. "Why don't you guys check out the street?" he told Allen. "Robert and I will join you soon."

When Allen and Bobby found an empty side street, Allen said that he had made up his mind to extend his stay in Korea for a third year, though he still had half a year to go on his present stint. Bobby had never even considered not going home when the time came to do so. "Extend?" he said to himself. It was an idea that immediately took the form of a possibility in his mind.

When Allen had finished half a joint and they were back on the sidewalk again, they found Mac and Robert in front of the bar, arguing with two girls. Robert had retrieved, from the bottom of his amazing dictionary bag, a portable typewriter he'd been wanting to sell, and he was letting one of the girls know how much it was worth.

"All right," he was saying, "let's go down there, then. If the guy's open we'll see how much he'll give us for it."

"I thought you were going to pay for everything," Allen said to Mac, but then he looked at Robert. "Good Christ," he said quickly, "it's your Olivetti," and he reached over and took the typewriter out of Robert's hands.

The girl looked from one man to the other. She was about sixteen and was having trouble maneuvering in her high-heeled shoes.

"Let's go back inside," Bobby said to Mac. "I want to see how Miss Moon's getting along."

Mac looked at the two girls, but then he said OK, and as they left Robert and Allen were arguing, the typewriter being pulled back and forth between them.

When they got to the table, Ron and Miss Moon were gone, but Ron's friends stopped Bobby's rising alarm by pointing and having him turn around. Miss Moon and Ron, of course, were dancing. The music was slow and the two were pressed together just like all the other couples on the floor.

When the song ended, Ron came back and sat down beside Bobby.

"Look," he said, motioning to Miss Moon standing a few steps away, "I'd be happy to take care of this girl. She needs someone right now. She doesn't want to go back to her village and she's not for you, right?"

Bobby looked at him and thought of Cherry. What he was after now was the cultivation of a life of his own, not a dependency on the part of Miss Moon. "She just arrived," he said. "She doesn't know a thing about cities. It was a complete accident, even, that we came all the way out here."

"I know all that," said Ron. "Why do you think I'm interested in her? I've got a hooch she can stay in. It's a good place, and for now I'll move back to the base."

Ron was looking at Bobby as if he were Miss Moon's father. Bobby didn't know how they'd communicate, but he said, "Miss Moon isn't a child. She can make her own decisions."

"Good," said Ron. "Frankly, the only thing she was worried about was how you would react."

Bobby looked at him again. How in the world could he know that? But Ron smiled and stood up, and then reached over and pulled a bottle of bourbon out from under the table. "I've got a case of this stuff in my hooch," he said. "Why don't you take this one?"

So that, in a nutshell, is how Bobby lost Miss Moon, though, of course, she had never been his. He spoke to her briefly, but she was so calm and positive about staying with Ron that there was little he could do. He simply said good-bye and walked out of the bar with his bottle of bourbon and with Mac, who said good-bye too.

"I'm going back downtown," Bobby said. "May I borrow enough for a taxi? I'll pay you back tomorrow."

Mac was hoping that they'd all go down the street to one of the other clubs, but Bobby was tired so Mac quickly gave him the money for the cab. Just then Allen and Robert came back, with the same two girls trailing after them. "No one wants the typewriter," said Robert. "Christ, it was ninety dollars when it was new."

"I want it," said Allen, "I keep telling you that."

The two girls were getting restless. Apparently Mac had enough money for beer and taxis, but not enough to lend Robert what the girl wanted to keep him company throughout the night. Then they saw Bobby's bottle of whiskey.

"Hey," said Robert, "where did you get that?"

But Allen was quick and took the whiskey out of Bobby's hand. "Loan me this," he whispered, and when Bobby agreed, he turned back to Robert.

"OK," he said. "I'll trade you this bottle for that typewriter. You can sell the bourbon in a minute out here."

Robert protested for a bit, but soon the trade was completed and Mac decided that he'd stick around with Robert and the two girls after all.

Allen, however, now that he had the typewriter, and after he heard what had happened with Miss Moon, said he'd share the cab with Bobby and then asked if Bobby felt like stopping off somewhere to eat before going on in to bed.

As they were talking, a taxi stopped in front of them and they got in. Allen wanted to light the remainder of his joint, but Bobby pointed to the driver so he thought better of it and popped the whole thing into his mouth, chewing it slowly and swallowing hard. He held the typewriter on his lap and sat a little formally, staring out the window as they drove away.

When Bobby looked at his watch he realized that it was not yet eleven o'clock. Only last night he had been at Headmaster Kim's house, on another planet really, softly singing about the bald-headed bachelor and carrying on. He hadn't even understood Miss Moon's problem then, but now, twenty-four hours later, she was not only out of that farmer's life but out of his own as well. It made him wonder, yet again, what he was to people that they could discard him so. Was he so incapable of closeness that he could move through the lives of others leaving no trail, not even so much as that of a slug through a garden?

Bobby looked over at Allen, to see if he might mention such a personal thought to him, but Allen was busy with his new possession. He had found a piece of paper on the taxi floor and had opened the typewriter and rolled the paper in.

When he saw Bobby looking, he smiled. "I keep a journal," he said. "I write in it every day."

Bobby scooted closer and peered at what Allen was writing. The paper was dirty and torn, but he had rolled its clean side into his new machine and had typed the date up at the top of the page. After that he wrote, "I met Bobby Comstock today, when I was standing in the *yogwan* hall with Mac and Robert. Bobby had this Korean girl with him whose name was Miss Moon. She was beautiful and shy and had never been to Seoul before. . . ."

Allen looked darkly at Bobby, so he moved back across the seat, not meaning to intrude.

"I never miss a day," Allen explained, "no matter what. You should try it sometime. Keeping a journal helps you to understand what life is all about."

Innocence

≡≡ ≡≡ ≡≡

*Nine in the fifth place means: Use no medicine
in an illness incurred through no fault of your
own. It will pass of itself.*

The next day Bobby discovered two things: Korea has a higher number of geniuses, per capita, than any other country in the world, and he had tuberculosis.

When the doctor told him that because of his positive reaction to the skin test he would have to stay in Seoul for further testing, he felt no surprise, taking the news as if he'd been expecting it. But the further tests had to be spaced apart, and as three days grew to a week and then longer, a certain understanding began to take hold. If he, like his grandmother at home, was to be an exception to the family habit of early death, then this would be his proving ground. He could barely remember his parents' deaths, but they had been no more than a decade older than he was now at the time. What had they known of life before they died? Had they come to any of the conclusions that were hovering about him now, beginning to make him take notice?

Bobby decided that he would not succumb to despair

but would defeat the disease, making it a natural culmination to the beginning he had so tentatively explored all those months in Taechon, the beginning of his life as a man.

There was a Korean woman working for the Peace Corps, an exceedingly fine person whom everyone considered to be the real boss. Bobby hadn't known her when he'd first come to Korea, but now that he was at the office every day they were becoming friends. Her name was Mrs. Shin, her English was excellent, and she was proud of the Peace Corps volunteers who spoke Korean well.

One day Mrs. Shin brought Bobby an article in Korean, suggested that reading the article might keep his mind off his lungs, and said she'd be back later so that they could discuss it. Though Bobby smiled and assured her that he'd read it straight away, he soon discovered that the article was full of Chinese characters and written in an erudite style that was missing from most of the food packages and bottle labels he was used to reading. He had been concentrating on speaking, not reading, and this wasn't fair. But Mrs. Shin was gone by the time he realized the difficulty of his task, so to avoid embarrassment, he borrowed a dictionary and went on back to the inn to read.

The article was in a women's magazine, and claimed that two decades of hard research had proved that Korea was the world's leading producer of geniuses. There were photographs of several geniuses in the article: a three-year-old who knew algebra, a seven-year-old with the meanings of thirty thousand Chinese characters on the tip of her tongue. . . . Bobby had apparently gotten in on a latter stage of a series of articles, for the one he read spent no time discussing whether or not the research was accurate, but rather took issue with whether Korea's geniuses were in abundance because of the diet or because of something in the genetic pool. The writer seemed to think that genetics caused the geniuses but that *kimchi*, the omnipresent Korean cabbage, played a large part too, working as a kind of gray-matter cleansing agent, readying the brain for fine reception and for quick retrieval from its hindermost parts.

It was an impressive article, all the more so because Bobby could read it. There were statistical tables that showed how well Korean immigrants in America had faired in standardized school tests, and there were dietary evaluations of the brain power locked within various soups and stews, one dish tasty for mathematics, another a godsend for farming and mechanical skills. The article was serious but its tone was amusing, and Bobby was captivated. Here was a level of study that he had completely ignored. Reading! The charm of the spoken word transformed into careful thought, a new grammar in which he might find a pattern for his emerging new life.

Bobby read the article several times and waited to discuss it with Mrs. Shin. Maybe she was free for dinner, he thought, or at the very least she could find time for tea. But though he saw her often he could never catch her eye.

It turned out that Mrs. Shin had given Bobby the article toward the end of his stay in Seoul, for one day the doctor called him in and told him that he had run the tests several times to be sure, and that there had been no error. Bobby had tuberculosis. Some people were more susceptible to the disease than others, the doctor said, and Bobby's susceptibility came from an unfortunate heredity and the unfortunate situation in Taechon, namely, the grandmother in Policeman Kim's house. He was also recommending that Bobby go home.

When Bobby came out of the doctor's office, Mrs. Shin was there. "Tell me," she said, "how did you like the article?"

"I read it right away," Bobby said. "We could have talked about it much sooner than this."

"Ah well," said Mrs. Shin, "I've been so busy."

Bobby told her he was going back to Taechon and that he would spend his remaining Peace Corps time learning how to read.

"Come," she said. "I'll walk you down the stairs."

The building had two elevators, but one was out of order and the other was slow, so everyone took the stairs. When they got to the street Mrs. Shin said that she had to meet her husband, and Bobby asked if he was a genius, making her laugh.

"Far from it," she said. "He's an engineer." She then asked Bobby if he'd run into any geniuses in Taechon.

"Two," Bobby said.

Bobby offered to buy her dinner, but she said she really had to go. Then she darted off into the pedestrian sea, waving above the heads of all the geniuses, or of those whose diets were making them so.

When Bobby returned to the inn he checked out and headed for the station. There was a train leaving at seven that would get him into Taechon just before curfew, and since he had had far more money than before, his per diem for the past month of staying in the capital on Peace Corps business, he bought a ticket for the second-class car. When he stepped out onto the platform the train was already there. And though there were already many people in the third-class section, the one he and Miss Moon had used when coming to Seoul, the second-class car was empty except for a boy asleep next to a tray of hard-boiled eggs and dried squid. The doctor had ordered Bobby back to Seoul within five days, allowing him this trip merely so that he could pack his bags and say good-bye.

Bobby found his seat and automatically tried to take up as much space as he could, the habit of a third-class traveler, though it was clear that the car would remain empty most of the way down. On the seat next to him he had the four bottles of pills that the doctor had given him and a note for Headmaster Kim, explaining the conditions of his early dismissal from his Peace Corps job.

The train was still minutes from departure when Bobby crumpled the note up and threw it out the window. He would finish his Peace Corps term. That was a condition of his own.

As he sat there, Bobby remembered the answer he'd given Mrs. Shin when she had asked him how many geniuses he'd known in Taechon. He had said two. Who in the world had he meant? He thought of Mr. Kwak immediately, of course, and then of his son, Bo Peep. Yes, Mr. Kwak for certain, Bobby thought. He learned a new language every time he had a child and he always seemed deep in thought. But Bo Peep was another matter. The child's precociousness was nothing more than the kind of cleverness hundreds of children had. Who, then, was the other? Certainly no one he had met at school.

Suddenly the train lurched forward and the Goma popped into Bobby's head. The Goma was the second genius. He had mastered the English of Mr. Nam's book without a day of schooling in his life. At the very least, he was a genius of survival, a genius without portfolio.

So there it was. Sixteen months in Korea and Bobby was traveling home to finish what he had begun, with two geniuses waiting to help him see it through.

The train had moved out of the city before Bobby looked up and around the car to see who might have joined him. There was no one, only the boy who'd been asleep, the egg man, who was awake now and coming his way. "Eggs have yes," said the boy. "Squid have yes, tonic have."

Bobby had a pocket full of money so he bought four hard-boiled eggs and a bottle of liver tonic with which to wash the first of his medicine down. There was something about the boy, the way he'd spoken perhaps, that reminded Bobby of the Goma. Eggs Have Yes.

There were more than four hours left of his journey, so Bobby put everything out of his mind, took Mrs. Shin's magazine up again, and turned past the article on geniuses, looking for something else to read.

The seasons are very distinct this year. There is not a blend, not the usual few days of spring with summer in them, or summer extending its fingers into fall.

My children are preparing my *hwangap* party, which is to take place after the academic year ends. My wife and my daughters-in-law have been sewing for weeks already, and my eldest son, who must pay for everything, has bought me wonderful shoes and a hat.

Since I have looked forward to the end of my career for thirty years, it is strange that I am not now more excited. Of course I realize that it is the events at school and the situation of our American that have made me feel this way. There is too much speculation about the impending transfers of Mr. and Miss Lee, too much discussion of Headmaster Kim's firing and rehiring of Mr. Kwak. Were I headmaster, would I have done things differently? At first I thought my answer to that question would have been yes, but after consideration I am not so sure. And it is not my job to second-guess the headmaster; that is not my job at all.

Ah but the situation with our American, concern about him is certainly a part of my job. The headmaster, though he didn't see fit to let me in on the identity of the spy, wisely told me that our American has contracted a small case of T.B. It is a secret—at Mr. Bobby's request none of the other teachers know—but it is a silly secret, for all anyone has to do is open their eyes and look at him. When he arrived so many months ago he was built like a barn, but now all his fat has fallen into the air, and the man that has come out of it is frightening to behold. He looks like he's been scooped out. Who would have thought that such an ordinary thing as tuberculosis would affect a man so?

What I am going to do, I think, is this: when my *hwangap* comes and I am actually retired, I will suggest to the headmaster that I invite Mr. Bobby to retire with me, though he will officially have another term left on his obligation to the school. I would not propose such a thing if it were not a question of his health, but since it is a question of his health, if he agrees then he can join me in the countryside, where I will go to live with my son.

Think of it, since Mr. Bobby's Korean is now quite wonderful we can discuss the nature of the world and he can rest until the time comes for him to go back to America again. What else, after all, are friends for? If not for help in time of need, what does it mean for men to be brothers in the world?

Written in Mr. Pak's clothing store, while waiting for my first daughter-in-law to select material for my undergarments.

4302年   3月   8日

Influence

≡≡ ≡≡

Six at the top means: The influence shows itself in the jaw, cheeks, and tongue.

There was no substitute teacher at the school, so when Bobby's tuberculosis kept him away, Mr. Kwak was called back to work. Since no one had ever been hired to replace Mr. Kwak, the load for Mr. Nam and Mr. Soh had already been heavy, and with Bobby gone it was unmanageable. And no one seemed to see any inconsistency in Mr. Kwak staying once Bobby had returned. What better replacement for the spy, after all, than the man who had refused to take part in his capture?

Bobby had not told his friends, or Policeman Kim's family, about the disease in his lungs, but he did tell Headmaster Kim privately, without Mr. Soh around. And when he wrote the Peace Corps doctor telling him of his intention to stay, he enclosed a note from the headmaster, endorsing his decision. "What's the big deal?" the headmaster's note said. "Half the country's got T.B." Perhaps the doctor would try to force him out, but Bobby didn't think so. He would have to come to Taechon to do it, and leaving Seoul was something the doctor did not want to do.

All the same, Bobby took his medicine religiously, and during the last weeks of winter and beginning of spring he took up the gauntlet of Mrs. Shin, that of systematically learning how to read. So that he wouldn't leave holes in his learning, he started with readers from the primary school and soon he had finished all those of the middle school and was borrowing books from Mr. Kwak, who had so easily become his friend again that Bobby was slightly miffed. He had wanted Mr. Kwak to take his previous weakness of character as seriously as he, himself, had, but Mr. Kwak hadn't been surprised at all.

It was a snap, really, learning to read. With spoken Korean he had had to rely on the inroads that sound and syntax made across the ridges of his brain, and that had required social contact, but with reading he could use memory and study, the handy standbys of his college days. Bobby made flash cards of the twelve hundred Chinese characters he had learned and taped them to the walls of his room. During February he put himself on a schedule of twenty new characters a day, and in March he began writing on the ruined surfaces of the blackboards at school. Poetry, slogans, the diaries of Confucius and Lao-tzu; with these writings he mined the language, staking his claim.

> Without stirring abroad
> One can know the whole world.
> Without looking out a window
> One can see the way of heaven.

Though Bobby had recognized, coming back from Seoul, that the Goma was a constant in his life, he hadn't seen much of the Goma since his return. The Goma, however, had borrowed a dictionary and an easy novel, so Bobby knew he was studying too. And then, early that spring, a bad thing happened. The Goma was fired from the inn, for too much study, perhaps, and in the middle of the night as well. The owner beat him and shoved him out the door, but the Goma waited until first morning light before coming over the fence and reaching through the bars to knock on Bobby's window, asking him to pass out some hot morning tea. It was raining and the Goma looked worried. "This is serious," he said. "I've been at that inn for ten years."

The Goma followed Bobby to school that day, and since they arrived early, Bobby brought him into the teachers' room so that he could stand by the stove. "Soon the teachers will come," the Goma said forlornly, but when the first teachers did arrive, barely ten minutes after them, they were the vice-headmaster and Mr. Nam, and when the Goma saw Nam he was ready. He held out the English book, hoping to gain another moment next to the fire by giving it back.

"Thanks a million," he said.

"Ah," said Nam. "Page seventy-two."

Mr. Nam took the book and inspected it, surprised to find it still in one piece. "One good turn deserves another," he said, tucking the book away.

"Page one hundred," said the Goma.

With the vice-headmaster looking on, Mr. Nam pulled a chair over to the fire and sat next to the Goma. "How can you say my book is bad?" he asked Bobby. "Look how much he has learned." He turned back to the Goma.

"I'm sick, Doctor, what shall I do?"

"Stuff a cold and starve a fever," the Goma told him.

"Won't you have some more potatoes?"

"Enough's as good as a feast."

Mr. Nam was tickled pink. "This is fantastic," he said, and then he pulled the book back out and gave it to the Goma, this time no question that it was a gift.

When the other teachers arrived, the Goma got nervous and left the room. Mr. Nam, though, went with him, and Bobby could see through the window that he was tucking the Goma down in the bicycle shed, where there was enough straw to keep a body warm. And when he came back inside he was ecstatic. "For the love of Mike!" he said.

Mr. Kwak had slipped in by then and the vice-headmaster had begun his speech, but Mr. Nam was beaming, happy as a clam, hard evidence concerning the quality of his book right out there in the bicycle shed. And as soon as the meeting ended, he announced that he was taking the Goma home with him right after school. It was the Christian thing to do.

For most of the day the sun rode high in the sky, warming the edges of the earth, but though Nam went out to the bicycle shed several times, it wasn't until everyone left at five that he called the Goma out again.

"Buddy, oh Buddy," called Mr. Nam.

The Goma had been up all the previous night, but he recognized his cue and called back from under the straw, "The day's half gone."

"Up and at 'em," said Nam. "Rise and shine," and when the Goma appeared the teachers cheered.

"Buddy's coming home with me," Mr. Nam announced again. "Little Buddy, safe and warm."

It was still cold, so Mr. Nam threw a corner of his overcoat across the Goma's shoulders as they walked. Bobby was going out to Mr. Kwak's house for the night to take a lesson in Chinese characters from the genius himself, but things had worked out well—the other genius was going home with Mr. Nam. Though Bobby had never been to Mr. Nam's house, he knew Nam was single and that he lived alone, and he imagined that the Goma would finally have a room to himself, perhaps next to Nam's, perhaps across the hall or off to the side.

As Mr. Nam and the Goma walked toward town, Bobby climbed slowly up onto the back of Mr. Kwak's bike. Though Mr. Nam was gloating, it really was an inspiration, the good deed he had done, and a circle of teachers still surrounded them as they walked away. The Goma didn't turn to look back, but he was standing tall. And his arms were at his sides, proof that he wasn't rubbing his sleeve across the diminishing scab under his nose.

The Gentle

Six at the beginning means: In advancing and in retreating, the perseverance of a warrior furthers.

Bobby had not heard from the Peace Corps, but the medicine seemed to be making him feel better, so two weeks after he got back to town he left again, this time with his Korean grandmother, Mr. Kwak and Bo Peep, and Mr. and Miss Lee. It was the occasion of a festival in the town of Puyo, honoring the memory of three thousand virgins, girls who had jumped to their deaths off the Puyo cliffs in order to avoid being raped by the invading T'ang dynasty troops. Puyo had been the capital then of a kingdom called Paekche, and Koreans from the region were still fiercely proud.

In the interior of the province, Puyo was about four times Taechon's size. It was a pretty town, and since spring weather had arrived with them, the day was fine. Trees were aflower with apple blossoms, pink and white against the base of a looming hill.

The grandmother, who was in charge of the expedition, would have had them immediately work their way up to the top of the hill, to the spot where the festival was to take place, but Mr. Kwak and Bobby both wanted a chance to wander, to get a feel for the town before going up high. When they stopped the grandmother held her hands over her mouth to cough. As they stood there hundreds of people passed them, and the grandmother closed her fist and shook it. "If we wait, all the good picnic areas will be gone," she said.

But Mr. Kwak knew that there were bookstores in this town. "Perhaps," said Mr. Kwak, "you could go now and we could catch up later." He looked at the grandmother. "After all, you know the hill and have a better eye for the best spot."

The grandmother was pleased with the idea and snapped her hand firmly onto Bo Peep's shoulder, ready to set off. "If you're not up there before dark you won't find us," she warned. "And the opening festivities are the nicest."

Mr. Kwak gave Judo Lee his bundle and said they would not be long, that they only wanted a sense of the place so that when they looked down from above they'd have some feeling for where they had been. And as soon as the others left, he and Bobby turned down the alleys of the town.

Puyo seemed slightly askew, not knowable in a glance as Taechon was. Whereas Taechon had two streets, Puyo had six, and the pavement laid on top of the dirt made walking a pleasure. Yet though the people in a hurry were all on the hill, Mr. Kwak walked fast, looking for a particular bookstore and saying they could move slowly once inside. There were always good finds in the bookstores of towns like Puyo, he said, but such a situation wouldn't last forever. Established families were selling their books now because the society was turning modern, away from philosophical thought.

They had to ask several times, but these interior paths

weren't nearly so crowded as the main street, and soon they were in an old store looking through stacks and stacks of well-kept books. The owner hurried from the back when they came in and then hurried off again to bring them tea.

"You look there, I'll look here," said Mr. Kwak. "We'll find books for me and books for your education as well."

Since most of the titles were written in Chinese, Bobby was pleased that Mr. Kwak thought him competent enough to look through a stack on his own. Mr. Kwak disappeared behind a shelf on the far side of the room and Bobby picked something off the first stack, the one closest to the door. There were five Chinese characters along the book's binding, but though he knew them all individually, he couldn't make them fit together to make sense. Inside the book, though, was a page filled with English, and he found the following:

> No Man is an *Iland*, in tire of it selfe; every man is a peece of the *Continent*, a part of the *maine*; if *Clod* bee washed away by the *Sea*, *Europe* is the lesse, as well as if a *Promontorie* were, as well as if the *Mannor* of thy *friends* or of *thine owne* were, any mans *death* diminishes *me*, because I am involved in *Mankinde*; And therefore never send to know for whom the *bell* tolls; It tolls for *thee*.

Though the rest of the book was in Korean it was Hemingway, not Donne, and Bobby tucked it under his arm. This really was a find. A book he knew well would help him read it well, giving him only the language to worry about and not the makeup of the book's world.

As Bobby's eyes adjusted to the job of decoding the titles, he was surprised to find that fully half the books were foreign translations, stories of the ages written for the average Korean to read. There was *The Magic Moun-*

tain, slimmer in Korean than it should have been, and there was poetry, Byron and Keats and Pound. And at the bottom of the stack were ten thin volumes of Shakespeare, play after play after play. Who, he wondered, could have done such work? What men, during these years of Korea's movement away from itself, would have thought such a difficult task worthwhile?

Mr. Kwak came out to see how Bobby was doing and he had his answer. These translators were the men of Mr. Kwak's fraternity, his true brothers, gracing the peninsula like jewels, members of an age gone by.

When the bookstore owner brought them their tea, they all sat together happily, the books they wanted balanced upon their knees. Besides the Hemingway, Bobby had found a book by Jack Kerouac and a copy of *Great Expectations*. And for his part Mr. Kwak had found philosophies of the West and East, a book of Zen Koans in German, Nietzsche in Chinese, and an extra-thick volume of Twain, placed on top as if to show that what America had produced was important too. The owner raved about the choices they had made. He'd read them all, he said, and could vouch not only for their content but for the quality of the paper and bindings as well. Though these books were old, they would never fall apart. Though the paper had yellowed, it would not crumble.

When they stood to leave, the owner walked outside with them and pointed up toward the top of Puyo hill. "I will close my store before winter comes again," he said. It was an odd comment, connected as it was to the festival forming above them, yet when Mr. Kwak and Bobby left, the bookstore owner stood sadly watching, hunching his shoulders in the spring breeze.

They, on the other hand, were happy with their books, and when they got to the edge of the hill the spirit of the three thousand virgins was so much in the air that they stepped into the upward-moving crowd easily, walking quickly along. There were hundreds of people on the hill, hundreds more on the path before them. But though the path was generally wide, there were places on it that were so steep that Bobby could reach out and touch the ground before him without so much as bending down. They were climbing hard and high, sometimes pulling themselves up, and Bobby could feel the elevation in his lungs and wondered how the grandmother had fared.

When they got to the top Bobby slumped to the ground, exhausted. Looking back the way they'd come, he could see other people lying on the path, too tired to move. And the grandmother had been right—the top of the hill was larger than it looked from below. There were families and groups everywhere, staking territory under every tree.

"There is a spot in the middle that will be the center of all the festivities," said Mr. Kwak. "Perhaps they have found a place near there."

Bobby got up and followed Mr. Kwak through the intertwining network of groups, but he found it difficult to walk. This wasn't what he had expected. It was too crowded, too festive. There were even concession stands up here, and walking among the crowd were hawkers, guys with peanuts and liver tonic in baskets hanging from their necks.

"Look," said Mr. Kwak. "The dancers and the acrobats will appear here tonight."

Bobby had been looking down, but when Mr. Kwak took his arm he saw a large clearing with a podium at its center and various pieces of equipment stacked nearby. Policemen were there, keeping people away, but right at the clearing's edge hundreds sat tentatively, waiting to press in once the show got started. Bobby had never before been in such a crowd. There were so many people that at times he feared he'd lose his balance, falling among them and upsetting their feasts.

They had looked everywhere when a voice finally called to them.

"Hey! I can't believe! Over here!"

Startled by hearing English, Bobby turned his head quickly and sure enough, it was Gloria, sitting on a large blanket right next to the grandmother and the Lees.

"Gloria!" Bobby shouted. He was glad to see her and looked around for Gary Smith or Mr. Kim.

"Small world, ain't it?" said Gloria.

The grandmother and Miss Lee were smiling, and Mr. Kwak was glad to take his son's hand and sit down. Judo Lee was apparently so satisfied with everything that he had leaned against a tree and fallen asleep, and Miss Lee had opened a basket and was trying to make everyone eat. Once Bobby had introduced them all, Gloria took hold of his hand. "Gary Smith gone stateside," she said. "Mr. Kim still driving his bad-looking cab. Puyo my hometown. Come back all ordinary-like for starting over."

Bobby wanted to take Gloria away somewhere, to watch her eyes shine out from under her Cleopatra haircut and to listen to her talk, but they were seated in the middle of twenty thousand people, on the top of a mountain, waiting for a festival to begin.

When a hawker came by with makkoli the grandmother stopped him, making him wait while she counted out the money they had to spend on drink. "Give us seven," she said, "and a couple of bottles of cola for the boy."

Considering the great numbers of people, the festival seemed pretty well organized. While the man gave them what they'd ordered, Bobby noticed a dozen other hawkers nearby. And since most of the Korean women were wearing their best gowns, the top of the hill was resplendent with color, drenched in reds and greens, brightness everywhere and the sound of silk moving against itself everywhere too. Only Gloria, among all the women, was out of costume. She wore tight jeans and a halter

top, but appeared to be as much at home here as she had
been in the Vil or on the farm.

"Look," said the grandmother. "They're setting things
up. I think the festival is finally about to begin."

It was late and though the hill was already packed,
everyone knew that, come tomorrow, it would get a lot
worse. Mr. Kwak and the Lees, for example, were the
only teachers who'd taken the morning off, yet many of
the others were coming over on the evening train. When
the headmaster heard that Bobby wanted to attend the
festival, he'd insisted that he go early, and now Bobby
could see why. Soon, he feared, people might begin falling from the hill for real, pushed off its edges by the
bulging crowd.

But the grandmother was right. From the edges of the
clearing in front of them, men had begun bringing out
long boards and were setting up contraptions that looked
like teeter-totters. Something was going to happen soon,
and they all stood to see more clearly what it was.

"The T'ang-dynasty troops won't arrive until tomorrow," said Mr. Kwak. "In the meantime the virgins are
at play, dancing and jumping, free in the enjoyment of
their innocence, the last moments of their maidenhood at
hand."

The men who'd built the teeter-totters had lit six fires,
and all of a sudden a dozen girls jumped up from the
nearby blankets and ran into the clearing like athletes,
their skirts bouncing as they waved to the crowd.

"These are virgins having one last good time," said
Gloria. "For them morning is an unknown whore."

The crowd roared, but from what Bobby could tell,
these virgins could outrun most troops, for they soon
commenced to sprinting around the outside of the clearing, their long strides evident in their speed but invisible
under their billowing gowns. And when they'd run past
everyone three times, they suddenly paired off and

jumped onto the teeter-totters, two-by-two, only standing up instead of sitting down like American virgins would have.

The pairs of women must have been matched perfectly, for as they stood out on the ends of the boards, the teeter-totters came quickly to rest, stock still, with each girl standing about three feet off the ground.

Bobby had thought that most of the people around them were spectators too, but he soon discovered that not only had they been sitting among the virgins but among the musicians as well, almost everybody near them a part of the show. Five old farmers from the blanket next to them suddenly sat up in some kind of formation and began playing instruments that Bobby hadn't even noticed they'd had before. There were two different drums and an eight-foot-long *gaiagum*, and two men were playing reeds. And the music was so atonal and cacophonous that it locked everyone's attention on the stillness and delicate balance of the girls on the teeter-totters, who were suddenly looking so forlorn.

"Only true virgins can stand like that," said Judo Lee.

After the farmers' band had screeched into the stillness for a while, it stopped as suddenly as it had begun, and at that instant a slow kind of movement began among the girls. Though they appeared to be standing still they were bending their knees under their dresses and causing, ever so slightly, a dip and pull. Earthward and skyward they moved, and soon the whole hilltop began to sway, as if the earth itself could feel the T'ang troops on the march, a few hours away but unstoppable as the tide. The grandmother took Bobby's arm, and when he looked at her he realized that it was in order to keep her balance that she did so. The girls teeter-tottered in unison, and slowly, from the movement started by the bending of their knees, a certain acceleration took place. When the ends of the teeter-totters first touched the ground, each opposite girl moved slightly skyward as the spring from her partner sent her off the end of the board. And when she came back down, her momentum sent her partner sailing up and a little away, still standing up.

This event was something Bobby had seen depicted on calendars ever since his arrival so many months before, and it represented perfectly a carefree afternoon for virgins, though the shadow of the wolfish T'ang was at the door. And though the farmers' band had been quiet during the acceleration, it started up again suddenly in a plaintive frenzy of sound that tore at the sky but sent the girls up higher into it at the same time.

These six pairs of girls were jumping perfectly and no one was falling. Yet as the band played on, the distance between the bottom of the nearest girl's feet and that stiff tongue of a teeter-totter grew until she was ten feet above the ground and then twelve, and then fifteen. It was miraculous, but they could all see, between the girl and the board she'd left, the dark blue sky and the mountains to the west and the curvature of the earth beyond the mountains. Yet no one fell. It was as if there was no limit to the height the girls could reach, as if they could avoid the T'ang simply by flying away, fleeing into the fantastic air.

Bobby was stunned. What a perfect depiction of the human heart unafraid, of trust in friendship and in the assurity of things remaining as they are. The girls jumped and jumped, each face composed, no mark of emotion upon it. And when, in the end, the six on top flew off the boards as if heading for the moon the crowd went wild. They were like slow female rockets and their partners on the ground stood with arms raised after them, like family members saying good-bye.

Whether the girls turned in the air or not Bobby didn't know. Perhaps they did, but it seemed to him that they simply sailed off the ends of the teeter-totters and up into the darkness. And when they landed, unaided and alone, they were in a perfect line, like chorus girls coming from the sky, only their skirts puffing a little to break their fall.

For Bobby this was the performance of a lifetime, and when he turned to his friends to say so, they all had tears in their eyes, even Gloria, for the way Korea had been, when such things were possible, before the Chinese invasion ruined everything thirteen hundred years before.

It was so beautiful and sad that the crowd might have wept the whole night through had it not been for the farmers' band, who, as soon as the performance was done, forced a change of mood on everyone by screeching out an alleycat's version of a waltz. In a moment the grandmother and all the other old women were dancing nearby. Only the men sat now, uninvited to dance and brooding, in postures that foretold of how badly they'd fare come the morrow. God, it's magnificent, Bobby thought. Gloria was Egyptian in their midst and Bobby really could imagine a world full of battles, with nothing decided by any other means.

The dancing went on and on, but when the women finally tired and came back among them to rest, they smiled and took the arms of the men and let them pour more wine. And when they all settled back to sleep, a small fireworks show began in the clearing where the dancers had been. It wasn't much really, only six rockets shot high up into the night sky. When they burst up there, everyone could see the colors of Korean gowns coming down, and then six parachutes, like little rag dolls of women, came floating back to earth. At first it appeared as though the parachutes would land in the circle where children were gathered, hoping to catch one and take it home. But a small wind came up, and as if they were tied together, the wind took all six parachutes and blew them just past the edge of the hill where they sailed on down into the town.

Everyone went to sleep then, fairly early, a whole hill-top full of people waiting. The sky was high above the clouds and though Gloria took Bobby's hand, they lay as still as they could and listened, both of them imagining the steady motion, the rhythmic progress of marching feet.

The Caldron

*The image: Thus the superior man consolidates
his fate by making his position correct.*

The invasion started sometime just before dawn.
Bobby had not slept well. Exhausted from the
previous day's climb, he could feel a new aching in his
lungs, and the tossing and turning of the people on the
hilltop had given him the feeling of sleeping among a sea
of grazing cattle.

But when he was awakened by the warning system set
up the night before, the shouts of men stationed at the
hilltop's edge and the beginning moans of women, he
came to his feet with as much energy as he could muster,
ready for what this day would bring.

"*Aigo*, the Chinese are coming!" said voices all around.

The weather was perfect for an invasion. There were
no clouds in the sky, yet since it was still spring the heat
would start out easy, not deterring the invaders as they
climbed the hill. Still, Bobby remembered the steepness
of the climb and realized why those few Korean defenders
of so long ago might have thought they had a chance.

As soon as everyone was awake, an element of frantic

abandonment ran through the crowd until someone summoned all the men, restoring order. Gloria, looking even
more Egyptian in the virgin light, nudged Bobby. "That's
you, man," she said. "Get a move on." The gaiety and
the eerie quality of the night before was gone now, re-
placed by the sure and frightening knowledge that death
was close at hand. Even Bobby felt the urgency of it as
they marched off to fight. "The ordinary hopes of all
manner of men are put aside when there is war," said
Mr. Kwak.

There were thousands of people on the hilltop, but only
about two hundred of them were men. And the women
seemed to recede as the men advanced, so that when the
men looked back there was now an expanse of land between them, though only a few hours before the hilltop
had been so heavily peopled that there was no room even
to walk.

Mr. Kwak carried one of the books he'd purchased the
day before, an old Korean history. He had it open to a
page concerning the invasion they were about to try to
repel.

"It says here that the defenders of Puyo hill were made
up of a handful of poorly equipped palace guards and
another handful of conscripted militia, laborers and peasants who'd been rounded up from the surrounding
estates."

It was light enough now for them to see the men they
stood with and easy to understand that most of them
represented the militia. Among them only a dozen were
in costumes of any kind. These guys were the palace
guards and quickly began shoving the militia around.
"Hurry fools, there are boulders waiting near those trees.
Bring them over, one at a time."

Boulders, indeed, Bobby thought. The man spoke
roughly, but Bobby put it down to him trying to get into
the spirit of the thing, and when Mr. Kwak turned, Bobby

followed, just a couple of peasants doing their jobs. From below them they could now clearly hear the shouts of the invading troops. And though there had been no room the night before for anyone to move, when they looked among the trees now they did find boulders, multicolored and numerous and made of papier-mâché.

Except for the cumbersome quality of the boulders Bobby could have carried six, and he tried to suggest to Mr. Kwak that they take as many as they could, setting them nearer the hilltop's edge so that they'd be readily at hand.

"No," said Mr. Kwak. "One at a time."

Judo Lee, though he would have been an excellent boulder man, had been told to stand among the peasants who would pour the boiling water. It had supposedly been prepared on fires since the night before, but when Mr. Kwak and Bobby got back to the hilltop's edge they could plainly see that the water was cold. Nevertheless there were barrels and barrels of it, and Bobby wondered how in the world they had gotten it up the hill.

While the guards were busy shouting at the water-carrying peasants, Bobby took the opportunity to move closer to the edge, to look down and see what he could of any T'ang-dynasty soldiers close at hand. There were wagons down there, and people were coming from everywhere to pull T'ang uniforms from them. The army was forming before his eyes.

"I get it," he said. "Those who come early are the victims, those who come late get to be the Chinese."

" 'The hill was sealed off for the night,' " said Mr. Kwak, reading from his book again. " 'But the women and a handful of guards, hearing of the Korean defeats farther to the north, knew that the hilltop would offer them only temporary safety.' "

"Right," said Bobby. "Not enough food, not enough shelter either."

" 'The peasant girls of the town surrounded the palace virgins and all pledged to die for their maidenhood.' "

Bobby looked back at the women, who really were on the other side of the hilltop now, and wondered which ones were peasant girls and which palace virgins. Surely those on the teeter-totters had been royalty. Surely, too, Gloria and the grandmother would be their peasant protection, both of them chaste again.

"This is exciting," Bobby said. "When will the invasion begin?"

" 'The T'ang had amassed a thousand men,' " read Mr. Kwak, " 'and attacked the hill at first morning light.' "

When he looked down Bobby could see that there probably were a thousand soldiers now, but it had been light for an hour. And would they really fall when the boulders hit them, bouncing harmlessly away? What were the rules in this war?

"The T'ang are coming!" yelled one of the guards. "Prepare to die for Paekche honor!"

For a while the T'ang-dynasty troops tried to catapult papier-mâché boulders of their own up to the top of the hill, but the boulders had nowhere near enough weight for such a lofty ascent, and as soon as their foot soldiers began to traverse the path, the water men soaked them down with a perfect shot, a barrel of it on the heads of the leading dozen. Maybe they were fighting a losing battle, but it was fun. They would not make it easy, no matter what Mr. Kwak's book said.

For a couple of hours the battle raged. With their ability to catapult gone and their cloth-tipped arrows easy to avoid, the T'ang soldiers had no other choice but to savage the paths with their bodies, running up the hill five abreast. And when they did so the defending water men got most of them. Those with boulders were told to wait until the T'ang were closer, crushing their skulls when they saw the whites of their eyes.

God, the barbarity of times gone by! Bobby mused. Though they had lost no one and cheered when T'ang men fell, by the time of the second major attack, they were out of water and could defend themselves only with their boulders and their hands. This time the T'ang advanced quickly, and though the hill was as steep as it had been the day before, they were soon so close that the call came out for boulders. Mr. Kwak and Bobby stepped up to the hilltop's edge.

"Steady now," said one of the guards. "Aim well."

They waited until a group of about ten were within a few yards of them, and then Mr. Kwak gave a sign. Bobby did aim the boulder well, angrily tossing it down upon their heads. Unfortunately, the same air that had foiled the catapult caused the boulders to bounce off the head of the first man and then float way out from the hill, off to the side. That one man fell dutifully down dead, but the rest of them were up the hill instantly, even as the defenders raised their second boulders up.

Mr. Kwak and Bobby quickly retreated toward the area of the virgins, pulling boulders along with them as they ran. But though Bobby made it through the trees, Mr. Kwak was caught from behind. When Bobby turned, he saw a T'ang soldier raise a sword, Mr. Kwak holding up his history book as if it were protection. "No!" Bobby shouted, but he was too late. Though he threw one of his boulders at the man, crushing his skull, Mr. Kwak's eyes had lost their luster, the life completely gone from them when he fell.

Bobby backed away. That a man like Mr. Kwak could lose his life in such a battle had not occurred to him before. What about his learning? What about the things he knew? As he ran he mourned for Mr. Kwak, but got the idea of using his remaining boulder as a kind of mammoth boxing glove at the same time. He held tight to the closer folds of the papier-mâché and began to run the thing against the invaders, knocking them down and out en masse.

"Hey!" said one of the T'ang, "a man can't wield a boulder like that!" and though he'd been killed, he got up and limped back the way he'd come, looking for a referee.

Most of the defenders were dead now, but about twenty of them still formed a semicircle, their backs to the virgins, who were edging toward the cliff on the far side of the hilltop, the one from which they all would eventually leap. When the others saw how Bobby had used his boulder, they picked up boulders of their own, and the defense went on much longer than it would have otherwise. They were like twenty Samsons knocking away at the hordes.

But there were too many T'ang troops even for boulder-wielding men, and the virgins, sensing that their part in things had been put off for too long, began wailing so loudly that the defenders all turned to see whether some T'ang men might have slipped in around the side. There were three thousand of them, Bobby remembered, pushed so far back against the cliff's edge that it was possible someone really would fall.

Bobby tried to see Gloria or the grandmother, but could not make them out in the mass of women. And the T'ang now were everywhere. He threw his boulder at the closest group and then knelt there, dead tired, a certain resigned spirit overwhelming him.

"Well, well, don't this beat all," said one of the T'ang men, and Bobby looked up at the helmeted face of Mr. Nam. The Goma was beside him and smiling.

"I got here early," Bobby said. "I'm defending the hill."

Mr. Nam smiled as he did in the teachers' room and then raised his sword for the kill, but the Goma pretended that someone had shoved him from behind and fell against Mr. Nam so skillfully that the sword cut into the dust at Bobby's side. Bobby took the opportunity and stood, limping in amongst the three thousand virgins, who swallowed his entry with the quick opening and closing of their gowns.

Bobby could hear the roar of the T'ang and moved with the virgins toward the cliff. But the women moved slowly and he, by making a beeline, was able to get there first, over to the edge of the cliff just ahead of them. He looked over the precipice. Whereas on the town side the hill had been steep, here it was concave, its edge cutting in and down, giving a clear view of the river below, and of the rocks on which all the women had died.

There was a restraining rail, but the lip of the cliff was at best three-feet thick and Bobby was afraid it would crack under the women's weight, breaking off and really killing them all.

"Hold it," he shouted. "Don't come so close, there's real danger here."

But though he waved his hands and slapped the sides of his filthy pants, he was like a man on foot in front of a mammoth stampede. What could they possibly have planned, other than real death? he wondered. There was a sign on the other side of the restraining rail telling him that this was the spot of the original virgins' leap, but now, as the women got near, they turned, choosing another direction, though Bobby still shouted in front of them to the point of such profound exhaustion that his own death, right then, would have been fine. God it was strange to him! He was on his knees when very suddenly he felt like he was watching a marching band or a military unit on parade, column after column of them neatly visible in rows, marching in order, away from him now, and away from the dangerous cliff.

There was an area of designated death that the women would reach before the T'ang got to them, because this was all a dance. They were not running now but moving in review, though Bobby was the only one who'd broken through their ranks and thus the only one really watching. He would have saluted had he had the strength, but the women kept their eyes forward, their arms swinging perfectly at their sides. Three thousand women? he wondered. Surely there couldn't be so many, for they passed as quickly as if there were only hundreds. When the last of them went by, the T'ang came in behind, and one of them saw Bobby and quickly came over to take his life, a sword touch upon his shoulder, gentle as rain. And as his head slipped under the restraining rail he remembered thinking that surely real death could not be so much different from this and he thought, life should be lived calmly, and he felt himself let go.

Though he could hear sounds, he didn't move, and though his eyes were open, the blue of the sky seemed to come down and cover them like water. He could feel the three-foot thickness of the earth below and he could taste the blood in his mouth, and he could tell that the T'ang soldier was still standing nearby, waiting to kill him again should he show any sign of life. Such peace and comfort. Ah well, he told himself, there are things in life to consider besides longevity and there would be other lives for him to live.

After that Bobby dozed and the next thing he knew Gloria was there gently shaking him awake again.

"Hey G.I.," she said. "Pretty fine. Come on. Let's go."

Though he tried, he was not able to break loose from the mood that had overtaken him, nor could he slip out from under the restraining rail. It had all been so real: the war, the flight, the death of Mr. Kwak, and the march of the virgins to their own deaths on the rocks below. But it was, after all, still quite early in the morning and Gloria was telling him that everyone wanted to go back down into Puyo for breakfast. The afternoon train would be full, she said, and none of them wanted to brave it as they were.

So Bobby finally stood, letting some air come into his damaged lungs and bending while the Goma slapped the dust from his back. When they crossed the hilltop and started their descent once more, the land seemed as crowded as it had been the night before—more so, of course, with the T'ang soldiers and the virgins settling into the festive spirit again, straightening out their blankets and calling to the hawkers for rice balls and makkoli and beer.

It was difficult going down, and though Gloria chattered away, holding Bobby's arm when the trail allowed it and smiling in the morning light, his head was still full of the thoughts he'd had when dying there on that hilltop battlefield thirteen hundred years before.

People are won over not by coercion, but by unaffected sincerity. I have known that all my life. Every morning for thirty years I have presented that message, in one form or another, to the teachers in our school. That was my main job, presiding over the morning meeting.

A strong man does not rely on the outward evidences of success in order to form his opinion of himself, but on what he knows to be the true elements of his makeup. This is what I know, this is what I have learned in my life.

Today I presided over my last morning meeting, gave my last address to the teachers, scolded my last student and poured my last cup of teachers' room tea. Everyone was very kind. When the headmaster spoke of my leaving, he said that thirty years in the same school was a feat not soon to be accomplished again. Of course, that is because the transfer system is now in effect.

When the other teachers stood to speak they followed the old tradition, with everyone saying some little thing, so class was put off until first period was nearly over. And all of the teachers were unfailingly kind, even my enemies, those who are secretly glad to see me go.

Now it is 9:00 P.M. and I am still here, the cardboard box in front of me slowly filling with my small number of personal things. . . . I have been trying to make the day last.

It has occurred to me lately that men don't live long enough, I think not nearly long enough, and I will tell you why. There is too much to learn and we are too slow at learning it. In two weeks' time I will become an old man and will be looked to, by my family anyway, for stoic support in times of hardship. In other words, in two weeks' time I will be wise. But it really seems to me now that these first sixty years of mine, the first sixty years of any man's life, should be looked upon as the period of childhood, after which a strong and healthy adult can emerge for a good long middle age. That would mean that an entire life would take four times longer than it does now, say about two hundred and forty years, but that would be all right with me.

When the teachers were standing and saying farewell to me

today Mr. Bobby stood too. It was very quaint, very precious. His suit had been tailored to fit his shrinking body and the skin of his previously mammoth cheeks was sagging down like melted wax, but what he said was this: "Good-bye Mr. Vice-Headmaster, I have always listened to your morning speeches and tried to let them mark my day." That was all, but I am inclined to believe that I would be a wise man already if I could only bring myself to truly understand that that is enough.

Written in one of the first-floor classrooms, on my final day, by the light of the outside moon.

4302 年   4 月   7 日

Darkening of the Light

Nine at the beginning means: Without rest, he must hurry along, with no permanent abiding place.

As soon as Bobby returned from Puyo, his condition worsened. He managed to finish the school term, but though he was supposed to stay for yet another four months, in the end even the headmaster insisted that he not carry on.

The big news at school, however, other than the poor condition of their Peace Corps volunteer, was that when the provincial teacher transfers were announced, Mr. and Miss Lee were not on the list. Perhaps Taechon was already considered the end of the road, or perhaps the Ministry of Education simply had no idea how to handle dissidents, but for whatever reason, Mr. and Miss Lee were to continue teaching physical education at Taechon Boys' Middle School. Several of the other teachers were transferred, but the biggest surprise was this: when school resumed again there would be a new vice-headmaster, and the man chosen for the job was Mr. Nam.

* * *

At Policeman Kim's, the grandmother, whose health hadn't deteriorated at all since his arrival, took Bobby into the main room of the house so that he could call America, a final gift from Policeman Kim, who, though not at home, left a message that he was saddened by Bobby's departure and sent his best regards.

It took a long time for the man at the post office to answer his phone, and it took longer once he understood that Bobby actually wanted to call the United States for anything else to be done. But in a while Bobby was able to hear the distant sound of a telephone ringing, way over there in America, so very far away. He realized as it rang that he had not calculated the time difference, so he did it in his head. Five A.M. It was 5:00 A.M. in America.

"Hello," said his grandmother's voice.

"Grandma?" Bobby said. "It's me in Korea. I miss you." As soon as he spoke, his heart was in his throat, but his grandmother hadn't heard.

"Hello?"

"Yes, this is Bobby," he shouted. "In Korea."

There was a short silence, but then she said, "Bobby dear, how wonderful. When are you coming home?"

"Soon," he said, "next week perhaps."

"Yes, dear," said his grandmother.

It was so good to hear her voice that Bobby clutched the phone and shouted, "What's new with you, Grandma? How's Mrs. Nesbitt? How's everybody!"

"Everything's terrible, dear," his grandmother said. "This war has everything quite confused." As she spoke the line was suddenly distant, and it soon crackled so willfully that Bobby held his breath, hoping she'd speak again on her own. The next voice he heard, though, was that of the Korean operator, the man at the post office tuning in. "Hello America," he said, and then the line went dead.

When the day of his departure arrived and Bobby was

about to leave the house, the children presented him with their school photographs and the mother with a parcel of food for the train. The grandmother took Bobby into the main room again and put him on Policeman Kim's scale. In his seventeen months in Taechon he had lost ninety-seven pounds.

The family excused themselves from going to the station, saying that too many good-byes made a farewell hollow, so Bobby left them at the gate, waiting only until the station man arrived and loaded his trunk on the cart.

When Bobby got to the station all of the teachers were there. Judo Lee said that once he regained his strength he should continue judo, and Mr. Kwak gave him a set of books, an impossibly difficult history of the world, so that he could continue his study and become a well-rounded man.

Bobby saw the biting woman and slipped her fifty won, but the person he was happiest to see was the Goma, whom he hadn't met since the festival, but who, Mr. Nam kept saying, was doing very well. The Goma, according to Nam, had become such a serious Christian that even Mr. Nam's own good faith was constantly called into question.

When Bobby saw him, the Goma raised a hand and came over. He was wearing a well-tailored blue serge suit and was carrying a Bible and a tambourine. His hair was combed and his shoes were shined, and on his lip there was no sign whatever of his reliable old scab.

The Goma squeezed the Bible, holding it up as if to let Bobby know that the pages were tight, and then he gave Bobby the parting gift of a hand towel with an English slogan embroidered across its center.

"Good-bye, Goma," Bobby said. "I hope we will meet again."

"It is easier for a rich man to pass through the eye of a needle," the Goma told him.

When the train arrived, Headmaster Kim came forward with one last gift, a second-class ticket to Seoul. "Go in style," he said.

For once the train was on time, so Bobby climbed up into the second-class car and pushed the window open in order to lean out of it and wave. The Goma stood straight, clutching the instruments of his trade, but the rest of them bowed so formally that all the way out of the station Bobby could see nothing but the tops of their heads.

Thus his time in Taechon came to an end. He had infuriated the Peace Corps doctor by staying so long, but though he had not fulfilled his desire to see his Peace Corps term through, he nevertheless felt peace of mind. . . . Perhaps that, too, was caused by the T.B.

That should have been the end of it, but as Bobby settled back into the seat to rest he realized that he was not alone in the car. Gloria was there, far down at the other end and sitting low.

"Hey!" he said. "How did you get here?"

Gloria stood and moved down to Bobby's seat. "Big surprise, G.I.," she said. "Travel all morning just to say so long."

Smiling at him she sat down and opened the package of food that Policeman Kim's wife had made, seeing what they had to eat for the trip. Gloria wasn't anything like Cherry or, of course, like any other person Bobby had ever known. Gary Smith had been his friend, but he hadn't said good-bye, and Cherry was in America and Miss Moon in Seoul with Ron. And here was Gloria traveling all morning just to say good-bye.

When she got the package opened, she took the Goma's hand towel and placed the rice balls on it, all in a line. Beneath the rice balls Bobby read the towel's slogan, a fitting gift from the Goma and Mr. Nam:

"Sweet Home Sweet," the towel said.

"OK," said Gloria, "let's eat."

Well, my retirement party was a success, and I have remained quiet for more than a month now, watching the hairs emerge from my chin and upper lip, waiting until it is long enough for me to be seen in town. Of course I understand that a beard is not an independent thing, and that to devote care to it for its own sake, without regard for the inner content of the man, would bespeak a certain vanity—nevertheless, I shall wait another week or two before I go to town.

It is wonderful, being retired; all my fears appear to have been unfounded. I walk the paths between the rice fields, and I look off at the mountains, and I crouch down where two paths intersect, sitting back on my heels to smoke. I wear rubber shoes all the time and I smile at my grandchildren when they come home from school.

Though I have not felt sufficiently bearded to be seen in town, I have allowed myself an occasional trip to the beach and it was there that I met Mr. Kwak recently. He is an interesting man. Mr. Kwak had news of Mr. Bobby, to the effect that Mr. Bobby is now doing fine. Apparently the fight against tuberculosis is quite advanced in America, for after only a month he is on his way to a full recovery. . . . Even his skin, I was told, has bounced back, recovering from its shock and coming in to meet his flesh again. Those were Mr. Kwak's words, but I hope that they mean something less than they say. I hope, for example, that Mr. Bobby does not fully recover his girth and become impenetrable again. It was interesting watching him change as much as he did, and I do not want to believe that he could forget what he has learned and become again what he is not.

Since I am now old I have taken up, without embarrassment, the Confucian practice of consulting the *Yuk Kyung*, specifically the book of oracles. It is amazing how, by doing so, I am often able to shed light on my thoughts, pushing away the clouds. And it is a great entertainment for the children.

What I had in mind, by way of this, the first entry in my diary as an official old man, was to cast my yarrow stalks on Mr. Bobby's behalf. I thought of it as a personal way of saying farewell, and I would have kept what was written and sent it to him when I got the chance.

But though I tried three times, casting my yarrow stalks right here in the dust before me, nothing I got made any sense, and I believe it would be futile to try again.

So when Mr. Bobby writes to me, I will answer him by explaining, as clearly as I can, that a failed oracle means only that a man must cast his own stalks, using the yearnings of his own heart to influence the way they fall. It was stupid of me not to have realized that before.

And in the meantime, since Mr. Kwak has told me that he is writing to Mr. Bobby weekly, I have satisfied myself with asking Mr. Kwak to relay to him a message. I was very specific with Mr. Kwak, telling him that my message should be printed out in English. Had I been wise when Mr. Bobby was here I might have delivered the message personally, but I nevertheless know that when he gets the message he will think of me and he will understand. The message is this: The superior man reduces that which is too much, and augments that which is too little. He weighs things and makes them equal.

Actually, I got that message from the yarrow stalks a week ago when I was consulting the *Yuk Kyung* concerning myself, but I didn't tell Mr. Kwak that part of it. What Mr. Bobby doesn't know won't hurt him. And besides, the message is universal, don't you think?

Written in a hollow near my son's house, as I watch for the dust clouds of the approaching bus—evidence that my grand-children are close at hand.

4302年　5月　31日